Did they think I would oblige them by walking to my doom?

I folded my arms and defiantly continued to sit on the ground.

"Up, damn you!" A vicious kick brought tears to my eyes. When I did not move, a hand grasped me by the hair and jerked me upwards. Had I not moved, my hair would have been torn out by the roots.

The cliff's edge was a short distance away and every step I took had to be forced from me by a kick or a buffet, and the savage blows compelled me forward, ever forward, to where death waited. . . .

Also by
Sarah Farrant

LADY OF WINSTON PARK

A prisoner in a castle tells her own story—Is it a tale told by a madwoman—or a desperate reach for survival . . . ?

and look for

THE LADY OF CHANTRY GLADES
LADY OF MONKSWOOD MANOR

Available in Beagle editions

LADY OF DRAWBRIDGE COURT

Sarah Farrant

BEAGLE BOOKS — NEW YORK

First American Edition

Originally published in Great Britain by Robert Hale & Co., London.

Published by arrangement with the author and the author's agent J. F. Gibson.

ISBN: 345-26576-9-095

First printing: May 1974

Printed in the United States of America

A Beagle Book

BALLANTINE BOOKS
A division of Random House, Inc.
201 East 50th Street, New York, NY 10022

Lady of Drawbridge Court

ONE

"AUTUMN my dear, you must have a companion! It is unthinkable that a young lady of your station should venture forth unescorted, and I presume that you do not wish to be immured in the house forever?"

"But Grandpapa, Aunt Sylvia accompanies me wherever I go! Why should I need a companion?"

"You will not have had time to notice yet, of course, Autumn, as you only arrived home yesterday, but your poor aunt's eyesight is failing rapidly. It has always been weak as you know, but now I am afraid that it will not be long before your aunt begins to experience difficulty in seeing at all! I pray that I may be wrong in what I have just said, but you must agree my dear, that for you to have a companion would ease the situation considerably. You know how it would grieve your aunt if she thought her affliction was spoiling your pleasure."

"Pleasure? Oh Grandpapa, what is pleasure compared with blindness? Poor Aunt Sylvia! But when I asked after her health yesterday, she did not mention that her sight had deteriorated," I replied. "Are you sure, Grandpapa? She seems to move as lightly as ever: I should have noticed if there had been the slightest hesitation in her step, or uncertainty in her movements!"

"Autumn, you must realize that your aunt has lived in this house for nearly twenty years, ever since she wed your Uncle James. During those years she would have learned exactly how many paces would carry her across a room, how many stairs there are, and where every piece of furniture is set. We have not made a drama of your aunt's disability, she would not have it so, but privately I have instructed Mrs Wilkes the housekeeper to see that nothing is moved from its accustomed place. Should the worst happen and your aunt become totally blind, she will be able to move with complete freedom about this house without the fear of tripping or stumbling against anything."

"Oh I am so sorry!" I was shocked by Grandpapa's revelation. "The poor soul! How dreadful for her! Yet she seems so happy. I do not think I could endure the thought of living in perpetual darkness. How can she be so brave?"

"Because she is a valiant lady, my dear. But to return to what I was saying, you do see the necessity of a companion being appointed to chaperon you, do you not? I do not intend to employ some grim-faced dragon to spoil your pleasure: I thought a gentlewoman of perhaps your aunt's age, who would also be a companion for her. Someone with a little *avoir de l'entregent* and a sense of humour, to be accepted into the family and help you undertake the duties which in future will be yours."

"Duties, Grandpapa?"

"Of course, Autumn, and you must be careful how you set about them. With the utmost discretion, you must take the reins of the household from your aunt's hands and gradually become mistress here. You are my heir, but as you know your Aunt Sylvia has ordered the household since your Mama and Papa both died so tragically. Your schooldays are behind you now, and it is time you began to learn what responsibilities your inheritance will bring you in years to come. It is better that you start your lessons now, whilst I am here to guide you. The staff are loyal and trustworthy and will be pleased to see you take your rightful place: indeed, with Mrs Wilkes and Dixon the butler to lead them, I expect the staff could keep Drawbridge Court running like clockwork with no instructions at all, but somebody's hand must be on the helm. Somebody must give the orders, inspect the books, and pass judgement when a misdemeanour has been committed. These tasks will be yours, my dear, but I rely upon you to see that your aunt is not offended in any way, or made to feel useless."

"Oh Grandpapa, as if I should allow her to think that for a moment! I love Aunt Sylvia dearly, and I am filled with admiration for her, and the way in which she has accepted this terrible cross she may be called upon to bear. Trust me absolutely: and do just as you think fit regarding appointing a lady-companion. Now, is there anything else we should discuss?"

"No Puss, that is all. Do you not think it is enough for one afternoon?" my grandfather smiled. "You may run along now, my dear."

"Thank you, sir," I replied. "I will see you later," and returned to the privacy of my room.

I remained there for what seemed a long while, collecting my thoughts and planning for the future: a future so different from the one I had imagined only the day before. That was the day on which Aunt Sylvia had come to fetch me from my school in Brighton. Schooldays were behind me: I had completed my last term there and was now a fully fledged young lady. No: not fully fledged, I had yet to be presented at Court; but nonetheless, I was no longer a schoolroom Miss. A life of ease and pleasure lay before me: oh, how gaily I had chattered to Aunt Sylvia as we bowled homewards in the carriage, and she had smiled and laughed and entered into my plans for my future entertainment! Yes, my thoughts had been centred on myself alone: where I should go, whom I should meet, a completely new wardrobe must be mine. Utterly selfish: my welfare and pleasure of paramount importance, with no thought for anything else!

But how could I have known? There sat my pretty aunt beside me in the carriage; blue eyed and blonde and a little on the plump side, but that added to her attractiveness. My Aunt Sylvia is all that I have striven to be my life through, and all too often have failed. I have never seen her lose her temper, or heard her voice raised in anger: I am only too often guilty of these shortcomings. She is not clever in an intellectual sense, but she is wise and understanding, kind and charitable, a little dumpling of a lady whom I love as a child loves its mother. Indeed, she is my mother, the only one I have ever known, and as she had protected me from the hobgoblins which haunt childish dreams, soothed my infant fears, kissed minor ailments better, and given to me the precious gift of a happy childhood; so I in return would care for her through the rest of her days, I vowed.

The head of the household at Drawbridge Court was my grandfather, Sir Mark Kimberley, a widower these many years. He had been blessed with three sons, my own Papa being the eldest of them: the second was my Uncle James, husband to Aunt Sylvia; really, she is my aunt by marriage and not related to me by blood. My Uncle Harold, the youngest son, I had never seen. I had been told he was rather a scapegrace, reluctant to settle down to a respectable profession, and my ever indulgent grandfather had allowed him to cross the world to see for himself whether a fortune could be acquired with the minimum of effort in Australia as he had been led to believe; or whether it would be wiser to apply himself with a little more diligence than hitherto he had been disposed to show, in England. There had been one or two letters to prove to my grandfather that his youngest son had arrived at his destination, but since then, silence! Enquiries had been made, of course, but they had proved fruitless, and as all this had happened over twenty years before the time of which I speak, it was assumed that Uncle Harold should never be seen again!

My birth in a brilliant October, hence my unusual and sometimes confusing name, was the occasion for great rejoicing in the family: I was the first child of a new generation of Kimberleys, but as time passed, I proved to be the only one. After my mother had recovered from the momentous task of producing me, and perhaps to help her recruit her strength so that she could repeat the performance with commendable frequency, my father took her abroad for a vacation. It was in Italy that both poor souls succumbed to small-pox which was rife in Rome at that time, and so before I had left my cradle, I was an orphan! Aunt Sylvia and Uncle James had remained childless and so I became her child and she my mother, and our relationship was as close, if not closer, than mother and child in actual fact. Now our positions were reversed: I would become the staff on which Aunt Sylvia could lean, but mine was a more difficult undertaking because she must not realize that my attitude had changed towards her in any way. Uncle James? Dear Uncle James! So long as he could experiment in peace in his laboratory in the cellars, the world was well lost to him. Gentle, absent-minded apart from his so-called work, he could be relied upon completely never to notice that anything was amiss. No: that task was mine!

There was a light tap upon my chamber door, and I heard my aunt ask:

"Are you in there, Autumn? May I come in?"

"Yes, Aunt Sylvia, come in do!"

"What are you doing moping in here on a lovely day like this? Come, let us take a turn about the gardens. You have not yet seen the roses, have you? They are particularly fine this year!"

"Aunt Sylvia, you have been remarking on the loveliness of the roses and asserting that they are finer than those of the year before for as long as I can remember," I smiled.

"Well, so they are!" Aunt Sylvia laughed. "Put on a wide-brimmed hat of some sort though, the sun is quite strong, and you know how easily you freckle."

I did not need my aunt to remind me of this fact. Mine was a pale, matt complexion which usually accompanies the mane of auburn hair which I also owned: Aunt Sylvia admired my hair inordinately and told me often that it was my crowning glory, but I would far rather have been born a blonde, little and dainty as she was. Now that I had reached maturity I could look down upon the top of my aunt's head with the greatest of ease, but there was one thing in particular for which I had to be thankful: I did not put on flesh easily and so I was able to retain a slender figure with no effort whatsoever. My eyes I could wish to be a darker shade of green than they actually are: 'Cat's-eyes' my fellow schoolgirls had used to call me, but that was behind me now. Who in future would dare address Miss Autumn Kimberley of Drawbridge Court in the County of Kent, heiress of the aforementioned estate and a tidy fortune besides, in such a manner?

"There! Is the brim of this hat wide enough or do I need a parasol as well?" I asked my aunt. My chamber was quite a large one and as we were standing at opposite ends of it with a good distance between us, I hoped to gauge the extent of Aunt Sylvia's disability by her answer.

"Oh, bring a parasol, my dear. It is better to be safe than sorry: anyway, they always look so elegant and one never knows whom one may meet."

"In our gardens? Auntie, dear, I have no great wish to impress the gardeners with my elegance," I said. "Anyone else would be trespassing."

"Not necessarily. I should not be in the least surprised if the Bretts drove over to take tea with us. I have ordered it to be served on the west lawn. Peregrine is staying with them: he too might come."

"Perry is there? Why did you not say that we might have company? I must change my gown!"

"Nonsense! That muslin you have on is very fresh and pretty and you look quite charming!"

"Well, let me change my hat at least. This is only an old one."

The Bretts were our neighbours. Sir Hedworth and Lady Mary Brett resided at Brett's Folly: their land marched with ours, and Peregrine, Lord Dexter, sixth Earl of Waring, was Lady Mary's younger and only brother. Sir Hedworth and Lady Mary Brett had indulged me since I was a baby and I should be so pleased to see them, but if Perry was there as well my cup of happiness would be full!

My earliest recollection of Peregrine Dexter was of a god-like figure fourteen years my senior: tall, oh so tall, he was nearly a man grown, and I would sway uncertainly on sturdy short legs as I gazed up at his adored countenance. He would lift me up and toss me high in the air to cries of 'Do not drop her!', then he would seat me on his shoulder and tell me that I was his queen, and that he would obey me in all things. That was a bond between us and as I grew older in my childish mind I decided to capitalize on it: I commanded him to marry me and laughingly he had promised to do so when I was old enough to become his bride. Patiently I had waited for time to pass, but there he had failed me: what other young female can claim to have been betrayed and to have had her heart rent asunder at the age of twelve years? The day he wed another I lost my absolute trust in mankind; I put away childish things, and bitter were the tears I shed into my pillow.

That was the reason why I was sent away to school. "My love, I have summoned Dr Bird," Aunt Sylvia had informed me. "You are not well: no, do not protest! You are so pale and irritable, and your appetite is quite gone. There must be something wrong!"

This was true, but I would have died rather than tell anyone the reason for my apathy. I was adult enough even then to know they would smile at my 'little girl fancies'. The doctor arrived and pronounced his diagnosis of my malady.

"It is her age you know, Mrs Kimberley," he hemmed, delicately. "Young ladies do sometimes become a little anaemic when they reach the age of the patient. It is quite natural Mrs Kimberley, quite natural. These pills should soon put matters to rights. A change of air would also be helpful if it can be arranged."

So my broken heart had been mistaken for approaching nubility; but when the pills proved ineffective it was decided that I should complete my education at a select seminary for young ladies in Brighton.

There was no leisure for moping in this establishment. Texts and samplers, each bearing an improving legend, adorned the walls where pictures would normally have hung. 'Up and doing, little Christian', was one; 'Satan finds mischief for idle hands to do', was another. Reluctantly, I had to abandon the romantic notion of going into a 'decline': I was allowed no time in which to pursue it. In any event, anyone showing signs of an interesting pallor at Miss Aston's Academy for the Daughters of Gentlemen was liberally dosed with brimstone and treacle and asked, 'Yes or no?' How could one equate such mundane matters with a broken heart?

Gradually the pain receded and I was engulfed by the new way of life at school which I was forced to lead. I saw Peregrine Dexter sometimes when I returned home for the holidays and he was visiting the Bretts: once I met his wife, and now I am bitterly ashamed of the spiteful things which I had wished would happen to the inoffensive lady. Just trivial silly things which would make her appear foolish. Oh, how I had envied her poise and self-assurance: wealthy, titled, and wed to the man whom I still loved with all my being; but the poor soul had died in childbed after four short years, and the baby had only survived its mother by a few days. Perry was now a childless widower, but the worst of his grief was behind him: his firm mouth could now relax into a smile which made my heart turn over; the little lines at the corners of his grey eyes became more pronounced when something amused him and he laughed outright, and the sprinkling of silver at his temples against the darkness of his hair made him look more distinguished and handsome than ever!

"Autumn, you have been standing staring into your mirror for nearly two minutes! Is anything amiss?"

"Of course not. I am sorry, Aunt Sylvia, I am afraid I was day-dreaming. Come, are you ready?"

"What an exasperating child you are! Here am I, awaiting your pleasure and you ask me if I am ready!" Aunt Sylvia laughed. "Oh, it is lovely to have you home again, permanently. I can admit it now: I missed you so much whilst you were away at school. I always shed a little tear when you had to return to Brighton, but I have never dared say so until now."

"Why ever not?" I asked. "It would have been a comfort to know that someone else was weeping as well as myself!"

"Yes, and if you had known you would have persuaded me to plead with your grandfather to let you remain at home. No: I had to be firm! It was good for you to go to school and meet other girls, and your health now causes no anxiety, whatsoever!"

Together, my aunt and I left my chamber and traversed the thickly-carpeted corridor which led to the main staircase: this too was carpeted, although in times gone by my ancestors had been content to tread upon the ancient boards of then polished oak. The sun streamed in through diamond-paned casement windows; shining upon carved furniture, dazzling the eye as it lighted upon the suit of armour which stood sentinel at the foot of the staircase, and glittering upon the crossed swords and lances which now adorned the walls of the panelled hall but which once had been wielded with such stern effect in Kimberley hands when might was right, and to be squeamish was to be conquered and lose all. Drawbridge Court, as its name implies, is an old house, half-timbered, with a red tile roof and great twisted chimneys. Originally it was a fortified manor-house with a drawbridge as the only means of access across the moat which had once surrounded it: but those days are lost in the past. The moat has been drained, filled in, and rose bushes grow where once there was murky, stagnant water; doorways and french-windows have been made in the erstwhile impregnable walls; but although it is completely obsolete, the drawbridge must remain. Yes: it does look slightly out of place as it has nothing to span but rose beds; but then, it justifies its existence by giving a reason for the name of the house. One cannot have a Drawbridge Court without a drawbridge!

"Did I not say that the roses this year were the finest ever to bloom?" my aunt challenged me playfully. "You have not yet had time to admire the gardens in all their glory."

Glory was an apt choice of word: mid-afternoon on an early June day when the flowers had not yet had time to droop and wither. Every bush and plant was in bloom; each blossom attended by a profusion of buds which gave promise of more beauty and perfume to delight the eye and intoxicate the senses as the season progressed. The leaves on the trees were still fresh, and the sun had not found time to steal the brilliant green from the close-shaved lawns.

We trod along the tare-free gravel paths, through the rose-garden with its marble seats set so that one might linger there in comfort if one chose, admiring the loveliness of the flowers but carefully averting one's eyes from the cheeky bronze cherub whose duty it was to spout water into the fountain in rather too natural a manner. On then to the white garden, where every flower was without colour and all leaves were of a silvery-grey: across the south lawn with its herbaceous borders and over the rustic bridge which spanned a sparkling stream. The stream lost itself in the lake upon which pink-tipped water lilies floated but we did not follow it to its destination; our path led us to the west lawn where wicker-work chairs were set in the shade beneath an enormous chestnut tree.

Gratefully I cast myself into one and exclaimed:

"How hot the sun is: I am glad to find some shade! Well, Aunt Sylvia, there is no sign of any company approaching us, not even Grandpapa. It seems our neighbours have other things to do, and cannot find the time to drive over just to greet me on my return from Brighton!" I tried to keep my voice light, but secretly I had to own to a feeling of disappointment.

"It is just as well," remarked my aunt unfeelingly. "I have no desire that any company should see you slouch in your chair in that ungainly fashion. Sit up, do! Surely you know better than to present such an inelegant appearance to the world after six years spent learning deportment at one of the most exclusive schools on the south coast!"

"There is no world watching at this moment," I protested, but nonetheless I altered my position and how glad I was that I had done so for no more than a few minutes had elapsed before I saw a vision in lilac taffeta gliding gracefully towards us across the lawn: Lady Mary Brett, squired by her husband and brother. At this distance it was safe to allow my eyes to devour my beloved Perry. He was clad mainly in pale grey: high silk hat, stock, waistcoat, and tight strapped trousers; the rich maroon of his tailcoat and the sparkle of snowy linen at throat and wrist completed the appearance of the most handsome man I had ever seen.

"They are here!" I cried, and dignity fogotten, I sped across the greensward to meet them and receive the hugs and kisses of Lady Mary and Sir Hedworth and my darling Perry. The two elder members of the small party greeted me as I had expected, but instead of drawing me to him in a close hug as he had always done before and kissing my brow or the tip of my nose, Perry took my hand and raised it to his lips, kissing it as a gentleman should salute a young lady, with the greatest gallantry.

"I see I must no longer offer you a seat upon my

shoulder," he smiled. "My little queen of long ago has fled for ever: in her place stands the Goddess of Beauty! Welcome home, Autumn."

I had meant to impress everyone with my newly-acquired polish: the manner in which I could accept a compliment gracefully, turn a witty phrase, be completely in command of any situation which might present itself. Instead, I stood there mumchance like a fool, feeling a blush creeping up from my throat to gradually suffuse my face until I was as crimson as a peony! Forgotten were the amusing replies which I had so carefully rehearsed for just such an occasion as this, and all my usually ready tongue could find to whisper was:

"Oh, it is so good to be home again! Pray, let us all be seated. Tea will be served, presently."

The afternoon took on a dream-like quality but it is as fresh in my mind as though it were only yesterday. For the very first time I sat in the company of adults as one of themselves; a young lady who had completed her education and could now be included in the social plans of the others. Grandpapa joined us under the great chestnut tree as we refreshed ourselves with tea, dainty sandwiches and tiny cakes. Uncle James had reached a critical moment in one of his experiments and could not possibly tear himself away from his laboratory, but apart from him, every soul whom I loved was gathered beneath the spreading branches of the great tree above us: there was not a cloud in the sky: nothing to give warning of the shadow which was to loom so heavily over us and the tragedies which would deplete our happy party and were less than a year away.

* * *

That same evening the cloth had been drawn from the dinner table and dessert set before us when Grandpapa once more introduced the subject he had discussed with me in the afternoon. Dixon had departed from the room, taking the footmen with him, and as we had no guests, just the four of us sat in a snug family gathering.

"Sylvia, Autumn, this is a matter which I think will concern you ladies more than it does James. I have decided to engage a gentlewoman to be a companion to you both. The time has now come when Autumn will be invited to attend a great many social events, or I miss my guess, and this will relieve you, Sylvia, of the tiresome business of acting as her chaperon at functions which you had rather not attend."

"A chaperon? For Autumn? Oh Father-in-law, I am sure we have not the least need of one! I shall be only too delighted to chaperon Autumn wherever she wishes to go. I have been looking forward to it for years!" Aunt Sylvia exclaimed.

I felt a lump rise in my throat, and was thankful to remain silent and compose myself whilst Grandpapa answered her.

"My dear Sylvia, pray do not think that I should wish for Autumn to be accompanied to any social occasion by a person other than yourself, but I think I must have given the matter more thought than you have. It will not be long before Autumn makes her bow to society and drops her curtsey to Her Majesty. Now I have been making plans! As you know, I never had a daughter, but I know how to set about presenting my granddaughter to the *haut-ton*! Another thing, I do not forget that you were the reigning toast before you decided to marry this stick of a son of mine: what you saw in him I could never imagine!"

"Oh Father-in-law, what a dreadful thing to say!" Aunt Sylvia was blushing like a girl.

"Yes, Sylvia, and in my opinion you have changed very little since James brought you as a bride to this house. I should be most surprised if you were allowed to remain seated on the 'matron's dais' in any ballroom for longer than a moment or two. You have kept house here for many years: this first season of Autumn's will be an occasion for gaiety and I am determined that you shall have your share of it. With a companion to keep young Miss here in order, you can dance the nights away with a light heart."

Aunt Sylvia was mollified, but still protested:

"I am sure there is no need!"

"Let me tell you of my plans before we go any further," my grandfather said. "I have instructed my solicitor to advertise for a genteel lady-companion. He will interview the applicants for the position, and he will then select any person whom he considers suitable. These ladies he will then instruct to present themselves in due course so that you, Sylvia, and you, Autumn, may choose the lady you wish to make her home with us and enter our employ. You see? I do not intend to foist anyone upon you whom you may not like."

"Oh, I am so glad I am not forced to earn a living!" I remarked. "Fancy coming all the way here from London, just to be told that you are not suitable! After all, we can only select one, presuming that there is one whom we shall like."

"You are mistaken, Miss: it will not fall out that way at all," Grandpapa beamed at me. "No! You, your aunt, and I are all going up to the capital when the time comes. I thought it would be an opportune moment for you ladies to replenish your wardrobes. As you are not to be presented to society until next

May, I do not suppose you can manage on the few rags you have to wear till then. We must live through nearly a year before you set out to ruin me completely with your *grande toilettes.* James we shall leave behind: you will not mind, will you James?"

"I beg your pardon, sir? I fear I was not attending."

"Are you ever? No matter; it does not signify."

"Where are we to stay, Grandpapa? At a hotel?" I asked.

"No, my dear, we are to be Peregrine's guests. He is opening his town-house, and we shall stay there. Lady Mary and Sir Hedworth will be there too, so between us we should contrive to amuse ourselves a little as well."

"Grandpapa!" I cried. "Oh you darling, oh it will be wonderful!" I left my chair to hurry to his side and hug him. "The Bretts did not mention any of these arrangements this afternoon," I said.

"No, I asked them not to. I wished to surprise you and your aunt. You have been a good child, attending that school when I knew full well you would rather have been at home. Not once did you come whining to me about any difficulty you might have experienced there. Well, the work is over: now is the time for play! Your aunt, too, I think deserves a taste of gaiety. We can visit the theatres and operas, and although you will not make your début until next year, we can attend small dinner parties if anyone is kind enough to ask us. Perry has promised to show you the sights, so I think you can look forward to being adequately entertained; and with his sister as hostess I shall be most surprised if we should sit down to dinner every evening with no other guests present."

I made ready for bed that night with my thoughts in a whirl. All these treats in store just to introduce a lady-companion into our household! No: Grandpapa had said that he wished to give my aunt and me pleasure, and what could be a more delightful arrangement than staying under the same roof as Perry! I should see him every day: know that he was never far away. That was my only desire: theatres, parties, new gowns were incidental. The fact that he was ever near would be enough for me to endure with complacency a whole regiment of grim-faced companions, each one with two heads and determined to thwart me at every turn!

TWO

THE glorious summer sped by: one idyllic day followed another. My aunt and I attended local garden-parties, syllabub-parties, picnics, archery-meetings and learned to play the newly-fashionable game of croquet: my poor aunt had but indifferent success with these last two pastimes, I fear. Most early mornings saw me in the saddle with a groom in attendance. Aunt Sylvia did not join me upon these excursions, but as she had never been a keen horsewoman this was nothing new. My aunt did not share my joy of rising when the day was young to see the first of the sun's rays stealing across the wonderful vista spread before my enchanted eyes; touching every dewdrop with magic fingers until it became a glittering gem.

September was upon us before I was aware, and then the preparations for our visit to London began to go forward.

"I suggest that we take the minimum of luggage, Autumn," Aunt Sylvia said. "After all, we are to replenish our wardrobes completely. I think three trunks each should suffice for the garments which we will take with us. Just a few things to wear until our new apparel is ready. Now, do you think we should take Bertha, or shall Miriam maid us both?"

Miriam was my aunt's personal maid: she was teaching Bertha, one of the local girls, the mysteries of her trade so that Bertha would one day be a fitting personal maid for me. The younger girl was not yet very skilled in performing the finer tasks required of her, but she was willing, sensible, and I liked her well.

"Oh, it would be a shame to leave her behind!" I replied. "No: let her come with us. It will be a treat for her to visit London, and she will be company for Miriam in the servants' hall at Waring House. She will make herself useful I am sure."

"Very well, dear: of course we could engage a fully-trained servant for you whilst we are in London. Someone who knows how to dress your hair in the latest modes, and keep your clothes in order."

"No, thank you, Aunt Sylvia. Bertha serves me very nicely: she may be unskilled but she is loyal and trustworthy, and with Miriam to aid her I am sure that my person will suffer no neglect."

In high spirits we set forth. Aunt Sylvia, Grandpapa and I drove to the railway station in the landau as the day was such a fine one; Miriam, Bertha, and Watkins, my grandfather's valet, followed behind in a closed carriage. The heavy luggage had been sent ahead and as the journey we were about to undertake was not a long one, we were able to set out at a reasonable hour with no dawn scramble to throw us out of temper for fear we might miss the train. Drawbridge Court lay in Kent, some ten miles south of Rochester, where we should board the train, and once the carriage journey had been completed we would be in London in a very short space of time. To travel by rail was quite a novelty for most of the members of our party. Grandpapa was quite accustomed to travelling thus, so too was his valet; but I had made the journeys to Brighton and back during my schooldays by carriage, and Aunt Sylvia had only been in a train once before. The maidservants looked a little apprehensive as they were ushered into a second-class compartment by the much travelled Watkins: to ride second class meant one was not cosseted with upholstery and similar refinements. I would have preferred that we should all travel together in our first-class compartment, there was plenty of room; but I knew that my grandfather would not have consented to such an arrangement. Servants did not travel first class except upon occasions when a lady made a journey unaccompanied, and then a maid might ride with her mistress; but of course, I was foolish to be so tender-hearted. It was a well-known and accepted fact that servants did not feel discomfort so much as did their betters: they were immune to hard seats, draughty chambers under the eaves, endless hours of labour, and the occasional blow. Of course, one did not actually set out to ill-treat them, but they did not feel pain as we did who were gently bred. It was a comforting thought but one at which I sometimes wondered.

The speed at which we travelled was a little alarming at first, but Grandpapa informed Aunt Sylvia and me that mishaps upon the journey were unheard of: thus reassured, we found it most pleasant to sit comfortably and watch the world outside our windows flashing by.

It seemed we were no sooner settled than we had arrived in London, there to be greeted upon the platform by the Bretts and three attendant footmen clad in the Waring livery of maroon and gold. These three worthies cleared a passage for us through the milling throng by the simple expedient of marching shoulder to shoulder ahead of us to the station entrance; cutting a swathe through the crowd as neatly as a reaper cuts corn. Two splendid carriages stood immediately before us, both bearing the Waring crest upon their doors: behind stood a plain coach although its coachman wore the maroon and gold livery; this one was obviously intended to carry the servants.

Waring House, Grosvenor Square, was larger than I had imagined, though not so old. Built in the mid-eighteenth century it was of the style so favoured in those days and reminded me a little of our neighbours' house, Brett's Folly. Marble columns abounded on the ground floor and the ceiling of every vast room was twice as lofty as those to which I was accustomed. Oh, it was all very grand: gilt spindle-legged furniture upholstered in satin, a different hue for each chamber: mouldings and carvings and deep, deep carpets: tables which looked as though they might collapse if one ventured to rest a feather upon them, and statues of a classical Greek design jostled pot-bellied cherubs for place-room so that no nook, cranny, nor shelf remained unadorned. On this warm day in September the temperature of these immense chambers was pleasant enough, but how did one fare in the winter? Houses such as this were designed originally for warm Mediterranean climes: this one would certainly be impossible to heat!

"Perry asks me to express his regret that he cannot be here to greet you," Lady Mary said. "We shall see him at dinner. Now let us have tea, and then I am sure that you would like to rest for an hour or so. We dine at eight o'clock, it is the usual hour these days for London folk. There will be nobody at table tonight apart from ourselves. I thought that on your first evening here it would be pleasant if we just dined quietly, and then perhaps we can make a few plans later on in the evening."

"That sounds delightful, Mary," my aunt replied. "Actually, Autumn and I are only too conscious of our countryfied appearance: we should far rather spend a little time quietly until our wardrobes contain something fit to be seen! That will be our first task, and we rely upon you utterly to direct us to the finest modistes and milliners."

"I shall do better than that: I shall accompany you both. I am sure the gentlemen will manage to occupy their time whilst we are engaged on such pressing matters."

We took tea in the blue drawing-room: slightly smaller than the others, it was obviously used when the company was few in number; then we were conducted to our bedchambers.

I was used to comfort: indeed, apart from the Spartan bedchambers at school for all of my life I had known nothing else, but here was sheer luxury! Rose pink, white and gilt: the room contained no other colour. Panelled walls painted white and picked out in gilt, each upper panel containing a fine mirror surrounded by little gilt cherubs. The four-poster bed was adorned and draped as were the tall sash windows with rose-coloured silk. An ankle deep carpet of pure white covered the floor: each separate item of furniture was white; the chairs, chaise-longue, and little stools upholstered in the same rose silk as the curtains. Upon the dressing-table were scents and essences, brushes and combs, pins and hairpins. The escritoire was furnished with notepaper bearing the Waring crest and coronet and every other necessity for writing. A small bookcase contained several of my old favourites and some obviously newly published novels, and the other books within it looked as though they would prove interesting reading as well.

"If there is anything further you require, Autumn, just ring for it," Lady Mary said. "There is a small bed for your maid in your dressing-room, but if you should prefer it she can share a chamber with your aunt's maid in the domestic quarters. Your Aunt Sylvia's chamber is the next one along the corridor to this, with just your dressing-rooms separating you. One of the house servants will show your maid where to press your things. Now, I expect you would like to bathe. Hot water will be brought presently, and then you can make yourself comfortable and take a rest. I shall see you in the blue drawing-room at seven-thirty, shall I? We usually gather there before dinner when there is just a small party of us."

"Oh, the room is lovely! I am sure I shall be most comfortable, thank you," I replied.

She smiled, nodded, and left me to direct Bertha in the unpacking of my possessions: it shortly transpired that our two servants, Miriam and Bertha, were each allocated a house servant to wait upon them. Bertha was a little over-awed at first to find that she had such fine city folk at her beck and call, but it did not take her long to adjust to the situation and soon she was giving her orders with remarkable aplomb!

The dinner gown I selected to wear that evening was of white crepe, very simply cut and trimmed with blonde lace. Pearls were the only adornment I possessed but they were extremely fine ones; a seventeenth birthday present from Grandpapa, and as Bertha fastened the clasp around my neck I regarded my reflection in the mirror with satisfaction. Yes: I looked just as I should for a small dinner party.

There was a gentle knock upon my chamber door and Miriam entered when I bade her to do so.

"If you please, Miss, Madam says if you are ready she will ring for a servant to show you to the room where you are to gather before dinner."

"Yes, Miriam, I am ready. I shall come to my aunt's chamber with you," I replied.

Actually, we would have been able to find our own way: there was only our corridor to be traversed, a flight of stairs and the length of another, and we were ushered into the blue drawing-room to find the others already assembled there. My heart missed a beat as the gentlemen rose and Perry came striding towards us, hands outstretched.

"Welcome to my home," he said, kissing first my aunt upon the cheek and then my hand. "I am privileged to have the three loveliest ladies in London under my roof. Take warning, I shall keep you here for as long as I may!"

We dined in the small dining-room that night, although to me it seemed as big as a church: there was a soft-footed footman behind each chair, and a butler whose raised finger set them all to scurrying. I cannot recall what was set before us, I only know that course followed course until eventually the cloth was drawn to reveal another beneath it: dessert was served and then all the servants left the room and there remained just the six of us seated at the candle-lit table. Happiness was warm within me as I gazed at each well-loved face: I wished to catch this moment and hold it forever: hold it fast against such time as danger might threaten or evil come amongst us. What a stupid thought! How could anything harm us: were we not secure? Honour, dignity, wealth and comfort were ours: what could possibly snatch any of these things away?

* * *

Regent Street and its immediate vicinity was the only place where anyone with any pretension to fashion would consider shopping, and shop we did until I was weary of the whole business. Morning gowns, walking gowns, carriage gowns; afternoon, tea, and ball-gowns, riding habits and each outfit's attendant accessories. Gowns for every conceivable occasion; but although I was allowed to purchase whatever caught my fancy, my aunt was firm when the ball-gowns were shown to us. A daringly cut masterpiece in black lace was paraded tantalizingly before me: I could just imagine myself in it, gliding gracefully down the grand staircase at Waring House, with Perry gazing up at me from the hall below with incredulous adoration in his eyes: but no, I must have white! As I had not yet been presented it was unthinkable that I should wear any ball-gown that was not white; well, perhaps I might have that beautiful eau-de-nil gauze and that pretty lemon silk for private parties, but all others must be white: colours were not for me!

The expression of dismay upon Bertha's face was so comical that I could not refrain from laughing aloud when my new wardrobe began to arrive at Waring House. With reverent fingers she began to unfasten the ribbon-tied boxes, to gaze in awe at their contents.

"Oh, Miss, I daren't touch them, they're that fine! What if I should spoil anything?"

"I should have to buy something else to replace it," I said. "Do not worry, I am sure that you will manage splendidly. Remember that Miriam will show you what must be done. Be guided by her and you will not go wrong."

Now that we could appear in public without proclaiming to the world that we were country bumpkins, our entertainment really began. To my joy Perry escorted us on a number of occasions when Grandpapa and Sir Hedworth cried off, pleading some business appointment which it was imperative that they should keep. I suspected that the two older gentlemen found their way of enjoyment was vastly different from ours: they met a surprising number of old friends at these so-called business appointments which took place mostly in clubs that they had not visited for many years. Grandpapa managed to acquire a fine pair of bays on one of these excursions; and upon another, he and Sir Hedworth disappeared for the whole day, to return quite late; it was weeks before we heard that a steeplechase meeting had been held that day, and sly as schoolboys they had played truant to attend it.

I prevailed upon Perry to take we three ladies to Madame Tussaud's Waxworks, Astley's Circus, and to listen to the military band playing in Kensington Gardens. Aunt Sylvia and Lady Mary were a little uncertain that we should visit these placcs.

"Are you sure you really wish to go, dear? I have heard that the crowds of people who attend these entertainments are not always genteel!" Aunt Sylvia demurred.

"Oh, they sound such fun! Do let us go," I pleaded. "If Perry escorts us we can come to no harm!"

When nothing more exciting offered, we went driving in the Park and Lady Mary introduced some of her many friends and acquaintances to Aunt Sylvia and me: once Perry took us on to Gunter's afterwards to partake of the most delicious ices I had ever tasted: this was a most respectable establishment where a lady could feel completely at ease.

London was thin of company at this time of year I was told, but Lady Mary seemed to have no difficulty in finding the most charming guests for the three dinner parties she and her brother gave during the month we stayed with them. Several owners of famous names expressed their delight in once more being invited to Waring House, which had been closed for a number of years, and although I was a trifle nervous to find myself in the company of such great people, the gallantry of the gentlemen and the charm of the ladies soon allowed me to relax and behave in a natural manner of which they seemed pleased to approve. Only one lady aroused my dislike, or to be honest, my envy!

"Isobel, my love, pray allow me to present my very dear friends and neighbours, Mrs. Kimberley, Miss Kimberley, and Sir Mark Kimberley. Sylvia, Autumn, Sir Mark, this lady is one of my girlhood friends, Isobel, Lady Frost, Marchioness of Drakesland."

I made my curtsey to the most beautiful creature I had even seen: slightly taller than I, with a glorious figure, silver blonde hair dressed in the simplest of styles, and eyes the colour of the deepest sapphires. She was dressed in a close-fitting gown of dark grey silk with just a small train, and around her milk-white throat was a priceless single row of grey pearls. The elegant simplicity of her attire seemed to make every other lady present appear over-dressed, and standing there in my white tulle I felt positively juvenile! If I had been whisked back to the nursery at that moment, I am sure I should have gone with no demur at all!

"I feel I know you all so well already, Mary often mentions you in her letters to me. We keep up a regular correspondence, you know, although we have not been able to see each other as often as I could wish. You are enjoying your stay in London?"

As a young lady should, I allowed the elder members of the company to lead the conversation, contenting myself with making a reply when directly addressed. Just then, admiration was the only emotion I felt towards Lady Isobel, and when Perry led her in to dine I was still content: as the most important lady present it was only normal for him to do so. She took her proper place at his right hand, and from my chair half-way down the length of the table they looked to be enjoying the meal enormously. Lady Isobel was not only beautiful, she was witty as well, and there seemed to be much to amuse the diners seated in her immediate vicinity: the ladies rippled with mirth, and one gentleman so far forgot himself as to let a loud guffaw echo around the dining-room. We who could not hear the cause of such merriment found it rather frustrating.

After the meal, Lady Mary collected eyes and led we ladies to the yellow drawing-room, where we could gossip in comfort until the gentlemen joined us. My aunt and I sat quietly and I watched as the other ladies approached Lady Isobel as moths do a flame. She was as popular with her own sex as she was in mixed company, a rarity for anyone with beauty and grace such as hers.

"She is lovely!" I remarked to my aunt. "Where is the Marquess? Is he present here tonight, I wonder?"

"My dear Autumn, you are not very observant! Surely her attire tells you Lady Isobel is a widow!"

"Oh, I am sorry. She is so young, the thought had not occurred to me," I answered.

"Yes, it was a great tragedy. The late Marquess lost his life in an accident on the hunting field about four years ago. He was a friend of Perry's. Actually, it was through Lady Mary that the Marquess met Lady Isobel. He was such a nice man: I met him once or twice at Brett's Folly. Their little son must be about six or seven now, let me see: yes, he was two years old when his father died."

"And yet she seems so gay!" I observed.

"Well, four years is a long time, my dear; one cannot grieve for ever! It is only right that she should take her place in society once more. After all, Lady

Isobel is still a young woman, it is quite likely that she will wed again!"

"I would be surprised if she did not," I said. "With beauty such as hers, she must have a host of admirers!"

"Perhaps, although I notice that she still wears half-mourning."

"Agreed, but you must admit that black and dark grey are singularly becoming to colouring such as Lady Isobel's," I remarked.

"Autumn, what a thing to say!" Aunt Sylvia was shocked and I had the grace to feel a little ashamed, especially when the lady whom we were discussing crossed the room to sit beside us and converse with my aunt and me in the most delightful and entertaining manner, with not a hint of condescension. Lady Isobel was a thoroughly nice person, but when the gentlemen joined us I could not but feel resentful at the way Perry singled her out for his attentions and hardly left her side. When my aunt observed:

"Are they not a handsome couple? Oh, it would be so suitable! He a widower and she a widow with a young son who needs a father. Perry always wanted a son: one of his own, of course, but that would surely come later. The little Marquess would be in safe hands with Perry, one of his father's dearest friends!" I felt the poison of jealousy stir in my heart.

"No!" I did not utter the cry aloud, for which I was thankful: tight-lipped, I sat and watched Perry coax Lady Isobel to play the piano for us. With the minimum of fuss she agreed to do so, and in this too she excelled. Oh, why had I not paid more attention to the music mistress whilst I was in Brighton? Perhaps the intensity of my gaze caused Lady Isobel to glance up, but I do not think she could have read any malice in my look for she smiled and nodded at me in the friendliest manner.

* * *

Theatres, the opera, concerts, several times we were all invited to dine with people whom we had met at Waring House, and upon two occasions we attended what were known as ball-suppers. To me, these were the grandest affairs imaginable, but I was informed that they were very small beer to what I could expect when the season was at its height. Fashionable society folk were rusticating at their country seats, or those of someone else; some might perhaps be found recruiting their health at a modish seaside resort; whilst the more energetic could possibly be discovered trying to impress our excellent English standards upon the savage foreigner, to the latter's bewilderment and resentment.

We began to see a little less of Perry, although I cannot possibly accuse him of neglecting his duties as our host. In the evenings when we sallied forth in the pursuit of pleasure, I found myself looking for Lady Isobel when we had arrived at our destination: I was rarely disappointed by her nonappearance. Of course, she knew the same set of people as did our host and hostess, and it was only natural that she too should be invited to these so-called simple gatherings. She was always clad in black, grey, or various shades of mauve, ranging from the palest violet to the deepest purple, and always she wore her grey pearls. As a person I liked her immensely, but how I wished that she was safely wed or at least betrothed to anyone but Lord Peregrine Dexter! Had I waited so long and hoped so much, only to have the chance of happiness slip through my grasp when if it was not in sight, it was at least a possibility?

So now for the second time in my life I began to taste the bitter fruit of jealousy. If Peregrine was absent from our company at Waring House I began to suspect that he was with Lady Isobel; and often it transpired that I was right. Sometimes as we drove in the Park we would see her carriage drawn by matched greys; with her coachman on the box and her footmen up behind, all resplendent in their livery of grey and silver, and at her side in the carriage would be Perry! One evening I heard him say to her:

"I shall call upon you tomorrow morning, Isobel. Will eleven o'clock be too early?"

"No, Peregrine, that will suit me very well," was her reply.

Before my first season had even begun I discovered that I preferred our life in the country to that which we were supposed to be enjoying in London. Poor Grandpapa: his carefully planned treat had become a penance to be lived through for me now. It had all gone wrong, and I wanted nothing so much as to go home!

* * *

It came as rather a surprise to my aunt and me when Grandpapa said at breakfast a few days before our departure for Drawbridge Court:

"Sylvia, Autumn, I trust you have not made any arrangements for this morning? I am sorry, I meant to tell you sooner but it quite slipped from my mind, that the lady-companions who have been selected as suitable by my solicitor will call upon you this morning. You recall that you are to choose the one whom you consider you like best to join our household?"

My aunt and I both stared at him and then at each other. I could tell from Aunt Sylvia's expression that she had forgotten the whole matter as completely as I had! She and I had been so busy lately that the thought of lady-companions had not even entered our heads!

"No, sir, we have no engagements for this morning, have we, Autumn?" Aunt Sylvia recovered herself first. "At what hour can we expect these ladies to arrive?"

"There will be four of them, and I have instructed that they shall call at half-hourly intervals starting at ten o'clock. I trust you will see them all, but do not make your decision known to them if you please. I wish for you to inform me later, and I in turn will instruct the solicitor. He will make arrangements for the chosen lady to join us when we have returned home."

This was the first time I had ever engaged a servant, for although the lady selected must meet with my aunt's approval as well as mine, I knew I should have my way when it came to the final choice. There was a small ante-room which led off one of the saloons on the ground floor: this I suggested would be suitable for the interviews.

"The other chambers are a little overpowering for anyone not used to grandeur," I observed. "We wish for these ladies to behave in a natural manner; after all, we shall have to live with one of them, and how else can we judge?"

"I fail to see how we can be expected to judge at all in the half-hour allotted to each applicant," Aunt Sylvia remarked. "Any one of them might have the most irritating habits of which we can know nothing until they actually take up their duties."

"Well, we shall have to do our best. There might be

a person amongst them whom we shall like at once." I tried to sound more confident than I felt.

"Perhaps. Anyway, a lady-companion can always be dismissed if she does not please us," my aunt said doubtfully. "Although it might be a trifle awkward unless she does something really wrong. These poor females are, after all, ladies! They are well-bred, well-educated, and each one has an impeccable reference. Oh dear, it is all very worrying! Just think, it is only through force of financial circumstance that they well be here at all! It might be you or me!"

I felt sorry for the first two would-be lady-companions, but they really were impossible. One ended every sentence she uttered with a giggle or a titter: nerves perhaps, but she exasperated me beyond measure: the other positively fawned upon my aunt and me in a manner which I found embarrassing. A person can be respectful without being actually servile; and if I had kicked her, I am sure she would have said that I did so in the most delightful way conceivable.

After we had seen these two my spirits began to rise, and I thought I detected a gleam of hope in my aunt's eye as well. If the third and fourth ladies were as impossible as the first two, we might evade the issue altogether for the time being and return to Drawbridge Court unencumbered by a person who would be with us for practically every waking hour for a very long time to come. Grandpapa would not wish for us to engage anyone whom we did not really like!

"Miss Phoebe Johnson, Madam."

"Come in, Miss Johnson. Pray be seated," Aunt Sylvia said, and carefully I studied the lady taking her place before us. She was small and dark with a few threads of silver in her hair and I thought then that a good meal or two would not come amiss so far as Miss Phoebe Johnson was concerned. Her gaze was direct and she seemed perfectly composed in our presence; seemingly unaware of the shabbiness of her well-brushed gown and the tiny darn in her glove, and even managed to smile occasionally. I liked her voice, well modulated; her replies to my aunt's searching questions given in a pleasingly natural manner, and only by the tense way in which she kept her hands clasped in her lap did she betray that obtaining this position was of paramount importance to her. Yes; I liked her! If lady-companion we must have, this was the one for me!

"You will be informed of our decision in due course, Miss Johnson. Thank you for calling upon us." Aunt Sylvia nodded dismissal, and I wondered how it would feel to hear those same words spoken to myself; then to await the postman every morning, and perhaps to pray for a favourable reply. I would ask Grandpapa to expedite the matter, I decided.

"What do you think, Autumn?" Aunt Sylvia asked when Miss Johnson had gone.

"I think that Miss Johnson should suit us very well," I replied. "Are you in agreement with me?"

"Yes, she appeared a very pleasant person. Well, let us see the remaining lady, although it seems we are decided upon Miss Johnson. We must see the last one: it is only right that we should!"

"Mrs Helen Ambrose, Madam."

"Come in, Mrs Ambrose. Do pray be seated."

The other applicants for the position had been spinsters: Mrs Ambrose was the only widow, and she was as different from them in every other particular as she could possibly be! Tall, statuesque even, dark haired and blue eyed; here was a lady who knew the world and its ways! She had travelled extensively and had also made her home in South Africa for a number of years. Mrs Ambrose was elegantly clad in pale blue merino, gown and round pelerine of the same cloth, and upon her head was a fashionable hat; black chip straw with what once had been a poor little bird sitting jauntily on the brim. Although she did not presume to lead the conversation, her remarks and her replies to my aunt's questions I found highly amusing. Mrs Ambrose was used to mixing with the best people on an equal footing, and only the untimely demise of a spendthrift spouse had forced her to seek a means to earn her bread. The late Mr Ambrose had gambled away his own fortune and the tidy sum which she had brought to the marriage, but she accepted life's buffets in a truly philosophical way.

"So Mrs Kimberley, Miss Kimberley, I am left to make my own way in the world. It is no use repining: there are plenty of people worse off than I. True, it is difficult at times to adjust to my new circumstances, but life is what we make it, is it not?"

Mrs Ambrose would make a most agreeable companion: to be chaperoned by her would add to one's enjoyment, rather than detract from it. She was full of vivacity, and in a very short while she was telling us a little of her life abroad, and of some amusing things which had happened to her late husband and herself. The time sped by and we were startled to hear the little clock upon the mantel-shelf chime midday.

Aunt Sylvia repeated her words of dismissal to Mrs Ambrose:

"Thank you for calling upon us, Mrs Ambrose. You will be apprised of our decision in due course."

As my aunt said, it was most difficult to choose between Miss Johnson and Mrs Ambrose. The latter lady was gay, amusing, well-travelled, and as a companion she would be most agreeable, well able to take care of herself and anyone whom she happened to be escorting. Now Miss Johnson was a different sort of person entirely: retiring in her manner, my aunt would find her a far more suitable companion than I should. At the back of my mind I was considering my poor aunt's failing eyesight, and although I liked Mrs Ambrose for her gaiety and her refusal to submit to adversity, I preferred the gentler demeanour of Miss Johnson in a situation such as this. She was the more likely of the two ladies to be helpful in an understanding and unobtrusive way if ever Aunt Sylvia needed more help than she did at this moment. Yes: Miss Johnson it should be! We would accept her into our household at Drawbridge Court: give her a decent salary, plenty to eat, and a comfortable home where she would be able to live with dignity. I recalled her tightly-clenched fingers in their shabby darned gloves: those days were over for Miss Phoebe Johnson. I felt quite maternal towards her! Mrs Ambrose would manage well enough, or I missed my guess: she was one of those ebullient spirits who usually contrived to settle themselves very comfortably indeed!

THREE

OH, it was good to be home! I think that I must be a country mouse, for junketing in London was not really to my taste; though I must never betray this fact to Grandpapa. I knew that the promised season of next year must be endured: it was only fitting that a young lady of my social standing and expected fortune should make her début into society, and, of course, the main object of this exercise was to acquire a suitable husband. Yes: it was hoped that I should take my pick of the dandies who twirled their whiskers and flourished their canes; but if the young gentlemen whom I had met in London were a fair sample of what I could expect, I wanted none of them. I wanted Perry, but would he want me? Would any gentleman able to choose between Lady Isobel Frost, Marchioness of Drakesland, beautiful, talented, agreeable: and me, an untried schoolroom Miss with green eyes, red hair, and an uncertain temper, select me? The more I thought of it the more I became certain of the answer. It was no!

One good thing came of our visit to London. I was able to gather the reins of the household into my own hands far less obtrusively than if we had not been away at all. Not completely at first, but daily I took on an extra duty here, an added responsibility there.

"Let me go through the household accounts with Mrs Wilkes and Dixon," I said to Aunt Sylvia. "Let me practise my arithmetic so painfully acquired at school."

"Very well, dear. I detest the task, as you well know."

Actually, figures came easily to me and this chore was completed in far less time than was usual at Drawbridge Court.

"You cannot be finished already, Autumn! Is there something which you do not understand?" my aunt enquired.

"No, thank you. Everything was most straightforward today," I replied. "Not like on some of the occasions with which you have had to deal."

"Even so, you have worked rapidly!"

"Oh, do not expect me to be so quick every time, or you will be sadly disappointed."

I chided myself for my foolishness: how stupid of me to let my aunt know that tasks which were difficult for her to undertake were simple for me! It would not occur again.

"Have you decided which chamber we should give Miss Johnson?" I asked my aunt. "She will be here by the end of the week."

"I had not considered the matter. Do you think that small chamber next to yours in the west wing would be suitable?"

"Eminently. Shall we go up and look at it? We must make sure that the lady is comfortable. Poor soul: I should not think that her comfort has been of the first consideration in her other positions. Miss Johnson must be so thankful that she was chosen to come here. Let us see what we can do to make her feel welcome."

Drawbridge Court is built in the shape of a capital E without its middle. The main part of the house faces south, and there is an east and a west wing. It is an old house, only three storeys high and on the ground floor are most of the principal rooms with just two drawing-rooms in the main front on the first floor; here also are the family bedchambers. The ground floor of the west wing houses the library, the gun-room, and a music room, whilst above these are guest chambers. In the east wing are the kitchens, the still-room, bakehouse, brewhouse, and laundry. Above are the housekeeper's rooms, those of the butler, and some more rarely used guest chambers. The whole of the top floor of Drawbridge Court is occupied by either storerooms, lumber rooms, or domestic quarters. The main front and two wings enclose a cobbled courtyard from which the house takes its name; and the stables and coachhouse lie beyond, where once the moat had encircled the house.

My bedchamber is at the west end of the main front, and we passed it to inspect the room suggested for Miss Johnson. Aunt Sylvia had called it small, but it was only so in comparison with the principal chambers. The summer chintzes had been put away: all our bedchambers were hung with these during the warmer months, but now that winter was nearly upon us the four-poster beds were draped snugly in draught-defying plush, as too were the windows. This room was hung in a cosy hue of golden brown, and the carpet of a neutral shade was patterned with tawny chrysanthemums. There was a large wardrobe which I hoped Miss Johnson would soon be able to fill with decent clothes; two armchairs and several smaller ones, a tallboy, dressing chest, and a table or two.

"What do you think, Autumn? Will it do?"

"Splendidly! Perhaps we should add a writing desk, and we must instruct Mrs Wilkes that the fires in here must receive the same attention as the fires in our chambers. Do you know, I am quite looking forward to Miss Johnson's arrival. I wonder if she will like it here?"

"Why should she not, pray? Really, Autumn, I am surprised at you! Miss Johnson is to enter our employ: she is not likely to be difficult to please. Take my word on it!"

But Miss Johnson was not destined to take up residence with us at Drawbridge Court; instead came a letter from Grandpapa's solicitors deeply regretting the fact that the lady in question found herself unable to accept the proffered position, and that he had taken it upon himself to engage Mrs Ambrose in her stead.

"I did mention to Dawson that you two ladies had a little difficulty in deciding whom you should select of those two applicants," Grandpapa said. "Is this arrangement agreeable to you, Sylvia, Autumn? If not you have only to say, and I will send Mrs Ambrose about her business as soon as she arrives: suitably reimbursed, of course."

Aunt Sylvia expressed a mild surprise at this unexpected news, but pronounced herself quite satisfied that Mrs Ambrose should replace Miss Johnson. I too was not displeased by the change of plan; although I felt quite affronted that the lady whom I had intended to befriend and make comfortable should obviously feel herself independent of what I had envisaged as a splendid position for a person in her circumstances. Well, so be it! Her loss was Mrs Ambrose's gain, and perhaps would be ours as well!

* * *

My nineteenth birthday was spent very quietly with just a few of our closest neighbours coming to dine with us. This was at my request, and I think Grandpapa and Aunt Sylvia were secretly a little relieved at my choice of entertainment. With the trip to London only just over and still very fresh in our minds, it suited us very well to sit at table with our true friends, people whom we had known for years and held in high regard; and then to be brought up to date with all the local news and gossip over the tea-tray afterwards.

Helen Ambrose arrived, settled in, and proved herself equally as agreeable and far more tactful than I had supposed at our first meeting. November was now upon us with each day growing a little shorter, and Mrs Ambrose entertained us mightily during the long evenings by telling us tales of her travels abroad and of some comical happenings which had befallen herself and her late husband. As she talked she would seemingly absent-mindedly thread with different coloured silks all of Aunt Sylvia's available needles. My aunt could still see well enough to embroider provided the light was good but found some difficulty in performing this last mentioned little task. I had discreetly explained the situation to our lady-companion and she was as tactful as anyone could wish. She expressed a liking for reading aloud and could make the characters in a novel come alive in our imagination: her handwriting was truly elegant, and she it was who penned the invitation cards or short notes which my aunt occasionally sent to neighbours. In a dozen ways Mrs Ambrose made herself useful by performing tasks not usually undertaken by a lady-companion; but she was never encroaching, never put herself forward where her presence or opinion might not be desired, and in less than a fortnight it seemed as though she had been with us for years!

* * *

Although I was now nineteen and a woman grown, the Christmas-tide that was approaching with such rapidity is the last one which I truly associate with my childhood. Drawbridge Court seemed to draw unto itself the annual magical aura which surrounded the old house at this particular season from as far back as I could remember. Such a scouring and polishing was taking place: it was all quite unnecessary for Mrs Wilkes' eagle eye missed no speck of dust at any time of the year! But this was tradition, a presage of things to come! Everybody was in fine humour, and full of goodwill towards their fellow-man be they high or low, and even the stolid Dixon permitted himself an occasional smile.

In high spirits my aunt, Mrs Ambrose and I set forth on a pre-Christmas shopping expedition to Rochester. I felt particularly joyous for I had heard from Lady Brett's own lips only the day before that my beloved Perry was to spend Christmas with them at Brett's Folly. We should see a lot of them I was sure as there was a great deal of coming and going between their household and ours in the normal way, and every year the Bretts held a Ball on Boxing Day to which we were of course invited.

Before we set out for Rochester I had spoken quietly to our companion:

"Will you please make sure that you do not lose contact with my aunt, Mrs Ambrose? I know Rochester like the back of my hand, and if we should become separated in a crowded street, I can easily find my way back to the inn where we shall leave the carriage."

"Of course, Miss Kimberley, I will cling to your aunt as tightly as a burr! That way we can both be lost together, for I know the fair city of Rochester not at all!"

"Mrs. Ambrose, if you can travel Europe and find your way around South Africa, I very much doubt that you will lose your bearings in Rochester!" I laughed.

"Of course, all this is only in the event that we should become separated." Mrs Ambrose smiled understandingly. "But pray, Miss Kimberley, do not give us the slip for the first half-hour or so. I should like the opportunity of purchasing some little token for your aunt, knowing that she is not alone whilst I do so."

Was there ever a more amiable creature than Mrs Ambrose? Yes: I had deliberately planned to lose my companions so that I could make my purchases in peace. I am a swift shopper: if I see an article which I like and which I think is suitable for its intended recipient, I buy it instantly and then go on to something else. Unlike me, my aunt's fancy will be taken by something, but she is not content until she has inspected everything else of the same category offered for sale, and then she will more often than not purchase the first article shown to her.

With my patience intact and in brightest good humour I was able to find my aunt and Mrs Ambrose as tea-time was approaching. My gifts were all bought and safely stowed away in the carriage and I smiled smugly at Mrs Ambrose as we waited for Aunt Sylvia to decide which of two almost identical cravat pins was the more worthy of her attention. There were only one or two more items on Aunt Sylvia's shopping list which had not yet been crossed off, and I guessed Mrs Ambrose's influence had again been at work in making my aunt complete her shopping in what was, for her, record time.

On then for tea at The Copper Kettle, to sit in the glow of a great roaring fire; eating muffins dripping butter and sipping scalding tea, well pleased with ourselves that we had accomplished what harassed and heavy-laden people passing the windows of this establishment were still striving to do: the Christmas shopping!

Drawbridge Court put on its Yuletide party dress of evergreens and scarlet ribbons. Mrs Ambrose and I bedecked the house, and I laughed when I saw the suit of armour standing at the foot of the staircase had not been overlooked by our lady-companion. It might have lost a little dignity but appeared most festive with a jaunty sprig of holly in its helm, and the lance clasped in the gauntlets was decorated with a frivolous scarlet ribbon tied in an elegant bow.

We always dined early on Christmas Day so that the servants might enjoy a nice long evening of leisure, and it was our custom to exchange our gifts to each other just before the meal: but my gift from Grandpapa could not wait until then he told me as we sat at breakfast on Christmas Morning.

"I pray you will accompany me to my study as soon as we rise from the table, Autumn."

"Will not wait, Grandpapa?" I questioned. "What will happen to it? Will it melt or something?"

"I doubt it, my dear. It will not melt, but it certainly will not wait."

"Oh, Grandpapa, what is it? Tell me, do!"

But he chuckled in the most aggravating manner and would only say:

"You will see in good time, Miss. Now eat a substantial breakfast, for it will wait long enough for that!"

When we rose from the table we all, of one accord, followed my grandfather to his study; and once there I stood and stared in great surprise at a wicker hamper from which came mysterious rustlings. I untied the ribbon with which it was fastened, lifted the lid, and gazed straight into a pair of huge appealing brown eyes which seemed to dominate completely the ugliest, most wrinkled little face imaginable! It was the tiniest pug puppy: a light fawn in colour apart from a black mask, and with a small curly tail which began to wave hesitantly in an enquiring and slightly conciliatory manner.

"What an enchanting little creature!" I exclaimed. "Come then, let me look at you."

He was quite agreeable to that: it meant being lifted from the hamper, cuddled in my arms, and being petted and admired by Aunt Sylvia and Mrs Ambrose.

"Oh, Grandpapa, he is lovely! Thank you so very much! What is his name?"

"He is yours to name as you choose, Autumn." Grandpapa beamed at me. "That is a task with which you ladies can occupy yourselves for an hour or so. Here also are some things I was assured when I purchased him the little creature would need."

There was a sleeping basket, a blanket, one or two playthings, a collar, lead, and harness. The collar and harness were so disproportionately large compared with the tiny puppy that they were destined to fit that they were put aside until such time as they might be grown into. Our village sadler would be able to accoutre my new puppy in a very few minutes I was sure.

We spent so much time admiring the little dog that we had to make haste lest we be late for church. I left him curled up fast asleep in his basket by the fire in my bedchamber: Bertha remained in the room to keep him company when he wakened. She was one of those Spartan souls who had already attended the first service at our little village church, so that I knew that the tiny life which had been put into my keeping would be quite safe until I returned home.

The carriage conveyed Aunt Sylvia, Uncle James, Mrs Ambrose and myself to St Paul's. Grandpapa had elected to ride, and as the village was only a short distance from Drawbridge Court the carriage and Grandfather's mount could return home for the duration of the service and then come and collect us when it was over. There was no snow on this Christmas morning, but there had been a heavy hoar frost during the night: everywhere was white with rime which sparkled and glittered as the wintry sunshine lit upon it, and it was far too cold to keep the horses standing for any length of time.

It was in an elated frame of mind that I enjoyed the short drive to the church, my cup of happiness was full: my loved ones were close about me: I had received an adorable little puppy as a gift, the very first I had ever owned: it was Christmas, and in a very few minutes I should see my dear friends the Bretts and my beloved Perry! They would join us after dinner later on and spend the evening with us! Who could wish for anything more?

We were not exactly late for church but we were among the last-comers, and as we made our way to our pew I glanced at the one occupied by the Bretts to see instead of three people, five! I had been treading on air, but now I came down to earth with a bump. Somehow I managed to keep the pleasant expression fixed on my face, exchanging smiles and nods as we in the Kimberley pew settled ourselves, but it was with the greatest effort. Five people were seated in the Bretts' pew: or I should say four and a small one. Yes, of course! Radiantly beautiful, serene and composed, Isobel, Lady Frost, Marchioness of Drakesland, sat and smiled goodwill at me! Oh, why had I never thought of wearing rich, deep purple velvet? But if I had, it would not have become me so well as it did Lady Frost. Bonnet and cloak both of deep purple velvet lined and edged with ermine; combing elegance, sumptuousness, and an impeccable taste in dress which made me in my emerald green seem positively garish! Beside her sat a small boy with tasselled cap, greatcoat and muffler, obviously her son the young Marquess, and on her other side sat Perry!

It shames me to admit that during the service my mind was not so attentive as it should have been. The proper Christian spirit with which I had so blithely entered the church had deserted me completely. Were they affianced: secretly betrothed? Why were the Marchioness of Drakesland and her small son spending Christmas at Brett's Folly? They had never spent the Yuletide there before, there must be some reason for it, and wretchedly I decided that this was the one most likely.

We stood and chatted, exchanging greetings in the churchyard after the service whilst we awaited our carriages and the gentlemen their mounts.

"Oh, it is so nice to see you, Lady Frost," Aunt Sylvia said. "Pray allow me to present our new friend and companion, Mrs Ambrose."

Civilities were exchanged: the young Marquess favouring we ladies with a courtly little bow, watched fondly by his Mama.

"We usually spend Christmas with my sister and her husband, but they are wintering abroad this year," Lady Frost informed us. "Dear Mary and Hedworth were most insistent that we should join them this year for the festive season. They feared that my son and I would be a little lonely by ourselves in Drakesland Castle with only the servants whom one cannot really call company. Alas, they were only too correct in their assessment of our predicament, and my son and I were delighted to accept Mary and Hedworth's kind invitation."

The brave smile which accompanied these words should have brought forth a feeling of sympathy from any but the most hard hearted. Perry took her arm, drew it within his, and gently patted her hand; and my heart turned to granite! Poor young widow: bereaved in such an untimely manner: bearing up gallantly for the sake of her son! There she stood with quivering lips accepting the comfort of the only man I could ever love, a pathetic young widow! True she was rich as Croesus, as beautiful as Aphrodite; talented, charming, gracious, all the things I wished to be and was not; and to crown all she could elicit sympathy with just the flicker of an eyelash or tremor in her voice.

We parted until later: of course Lady Frost would accompany Perry and the Bretts when they visited us in the evening so I could look forward to further treats in store; like watching the man I loved comforting and dancing attendance on someone else. I had waited for so long and hoped so much, and here he was being taken from under my very nose! But what chance did I stand against her?

My puppy clambered with difficulty out of his basket and came waddling across what must have seemed to him a vast expanse of carpet, to greet me when I returned to my room.

"He hasn't stirred from that basket in all the time you've been gone, Miss," Bertha informed me. "He must have been tired out, poor little mite!"

The poor little mite was now quite rested and showed a propensity to play: he soon discovered that his teeth would support the weight of his body if he dug them with great determination into my skirt. To swing by his teeth from my gown as I walked might, in his opinion, have proved to be a fine game, but if I was to have any gown with its skirt intact this quaint form of amusement must be nipped in the bud. Gently I removed the little animal, saying in a stern voice:

"No! That's naughty!" to receive for my pains a nip on the finger from his needle-sharp teeth. He then ran under the bed and refused to come out until Bertha screwed a piece of paper into a ball and threw it on to the floor: the puppy then emerged to chase it, quite oblivious of the fact that he had offered insult and injury to me, his new mistress. I too soon forgot the incident as the game progressed and we eventually made our way downstairs for luncheon, the greatest of friends.

I had not named my new acquisition when our guests arrived for the evening. Hero, Midget, Gargoyle, and sundry other names ranging from the appropriate to the absurd had been put forward and rejected, but when Perry suggested:

"Why, Carlin, to be sure! Carlin is French for pug. It is just the name for him!" the choice was made. Carlin he became, and Carlin he has remained ever since.

FOUR

Now that the Christmas and New Year festivities were over, we at Drawbridge Court began to turn our attention towards the forthcoming London season. Perry had returned to his own estates in Derbyshire: Lady Frost and her son had departed whither I knew not; but there had been no formal announcement of their betrothal! I had half expected to hear this knell of doom at the Brett's Boxing Day Ball, but the evening had passed with no declaration of any intended marriage so the little flicker of hope within me still refused to be quenched.

As Grandpapa often stated that he did not believe in doing things by halves, it came as no surprise to me when he informed us:

"I have instructed my solicitor to look about him for a decent house to accommodate us for the season. Once he has found something worth viewing I intend to go up to London and inspect it, and if it meets with my approval I shall leave Dixon up there to engage staff and so forth. Our butler knows our preferences and requirements, and we can manage here at Drawbridge Court with Mrs Wilkes in charge for a few weeks."

"Do you not think we others should see the house before you engage to hire it, Father-in-law?" my aunt asked, diffidently.

"No, my dear Sylvia, I do not. I am quite capable of judging whether a residence will suit our style of living and support our comfort," was the reply. "Besides, I intend to spend two or three days in London. There are several things to which I must attend, not the least of these is to visit the coachmaker and order an elegant carriage to be built, perhaps a landau as well. I do not desire you ladies to drive to the Palace for one of Her Majesty's Drawing Rooms in a hired cab! The vehicles we have here are comfortable, true, but you must own them to be a trifle old-fashioned!"

These were Grandpapa's affairs, but soon I learned that a contribution of effort on my part was required as well. Like any well-bred filly, I must be trained to show my paces.

"Autumn, dear, I do wish you would practise walking more slowly," Aunt Sylvia informed me. "Your gait is far too brisk. Take shorter steps, I pray you: try to make it appear that you glide rather than walk. Hold your head high in a queenly manner: try to emulate the grace of a swan! No: do not thrust out your chin so, it looks most arrogant. And straighten your back, do!"

"It is so fortunate that Miss Kimberley is slender!" Mrs Ambrose remarked.

I looked on her with favour. Here at last was a laudable attribute which required no effort on my part whatsoever. Her next words completely spoiled this pleasant reflection.

"Yes, a sylph-like figure is such a gift from Mother Nature, but it does sometimes need a little help to show it to its proper advantage," Mrs Ambrose continued. "A tiny waist is so much admired! I remember as a young girl mine was a mere seventeen inches: alas, those days are gone! Perhaps if Miss Kimberley were laced a trifle more tightly? To start doing so now would mean that she could have grown accustomed to it for the approaching season."

"What a splendid idea!" approved Aunt Sylvia.

"Please instruct Bertha to do so, Autumn. If she cannot manage the task alone, Miriam will help her."

"I think my waistline is very well as it is," I answered, rebelliously. "It only measures twenty-three inches, after all!"

"So much as that? Dear me, that will never do! You would seem like an elephant beside the other young ladies who are to be presented. And that reminds me, you must practise your Court curtsey. Yes, I know you are quite graceful in the ordinary way: but then, a bow to Her Majesty or any other member of the Royal Family is very far from being ordinary!"

"Let me show you I am quite capable of making an appropriate curtsey and then we can have done with the matter."

Confidently, I placed myself where Aunt Sylvia could not fail to see me, spread my skirts wide, and lowered myself as far as possible until I was almost sitting on my hindmost heel. Yes: I have to admit that I did wobble a little, but that was excusable, surely?

"Now raise yourself, my dear," instructed my aunt, and with a deal more difficulty I did so.

"And you say you do not need practice?" demanded Aunt Sylvia. "Your back was as bent as that of an old woman! Your chin was nearly on your knees! You could not even hold your balance; and do not forget, you will be wearing a heavy train with which you must contend: there will be plumes in your hair, and you will be carrying a fan and a bouquet at least. Do you still feel confident?"

Daily I practised, and my aunt or Mrs Ambrose or both would come to my chamber to make sure that I did so seriously. With a heavy curtain suspended from my shoulders in place of a train: the shoes with the highest heels that I possessed upon my feet: my waist laced in so tightly that I could hardly breathe;

and a pile of books upon my head to ensure a graceful carriage, I paraded up and down my chamber like the biggest fool in Christendom!

Carlin was delighted with these antics: here was a new game devised by his mistress solely for his entertainment and pleasure! He would sit upon my improvised train and be borne along in grand style; or he would crawl underneath it, snapping at my ankles as I trod my dignified gait, or tripping me as I attempted to execute a graceful turn.

"I think it would be a good idea if Bertha took your puppy for a walk whilst you are practising your deportment," said my aunt in exasperation. "We are getting nowhere like this! Come now, you must try the stairs."

"What? Like this? The servants will think that I am out of my mind!"

"What they think is immaterial. Servants have no place to think, anyway. Come along now, we are wasting time!"

Everything must be done with the forthcoming season in mind: my hair received a hundred brush-strokes nightly? That must be doubled to ensure a really brilliant sheen.

"I have remarked many times that your hair is your crowning glory," said my aunt. "And I think a daily application of lemon juice to your hands would be beneficial: it is so good for whitening the skin! I remember when I was a girl it was quite the thing for a young lady to sleep with her hands tied to the overhead bed-posts on the night before a really important occasion. I never did so: my Mama thought it a trifle too extreme, but some young ladies would suffer anything for the sake of an elegant appearance!"

"What a great deal of fuss!" I exclaimed. "After all,

one is supposed to be enjoying oneself: otherwise, why bother?"

"Enjoying oneself? My dear Autumn, that is beside the point entirely! One enters society to see and be seen: to make eligible connections; and possibly to secure, nay primarily to secure, a husband!"

"Aunt Sylvia, I give you fair warning that I shall be a very difficult person to please. Not one of the dainty dandies whom we met in London last September would rate a second glance from me, let alone cause my heart to flutter!"

"We shall see, my dear, we shall see!" Aunt Sylvia and Mrs Ambrose exchanged understanding matronly smiles. Smile away, I thought. Yes, indeed, we shall see!

* * *

It was in late February when Grandpapa greeted us at the breakfast table with the announcement:

"I have heard from Dawson, my solicitor. He tells me he has found us a most suitable house for our stay in London, and he urges me to inspect it without delay. By all accounts, decent accommodation will be very hard to come by shortly. I intend to travel up to London tomorrow, taking Dixon and Watkins with me, of course. We will stay at a hotel for a few days, then Watkins and I shall return home and Dixon will remain behind to order the house to our liking. I am sure it will be suitable, Dawson would not have me chasing up to London on a fool's errand! Oh Mrs Ambrose, I have a letter here for you: it was enclosed in the one I received from my solicitor. From the many addresses upon the envelope it appears to have travelled many miles before it has finally reached you!"

"Thank you, Sir Mark. Yes, as you say it does seem to have lost its way to such an extent that I am fortunate to have received it at all!"

She glanced at the various directions upon the envelope, and then calmly laid it beside her plate as she continued to eat her breakfast. What strength of will: what perfect manners Mrs Ambrose possessed! I should have ripped open the envelope and at least scanned the contents of the letter if it had been addressed to me. It was the first one that Mrs Ambrose had received since she had joined our household I knew; and here she was, calmly spooning her egg as though it was an everyday occurrence!

A wind that was nearly of gale force blew for all of that day, bearing with it rain. It may seem unusual to recall the weather so clearly, but this was a day which I shall remember for the rest of my life. As evening approached, the wind still whined about the house: buffeting the windows and causing unsecured doors to bang; but the rain which had fallen for most of the day had ceased although the sky was still full of scurrying cloud.

As we gathered for dinner I was startled to see Grandpapa dressed for riding instead of his normal evening attire. He saw me looking askance at him and chuckled.

"Ladies," he said. "I beg you to excuse my dress at the dinner table tonight. I have formed the intention of riding over to Brett's Folly a little later on. Sir Hedworth may have some commission which he wishes me to execute whilst I am in London, and it would be most unneighbourly for me to set off without asking if this is so."

"But it will be completely dark by then, Grandpapa!" I exclaimed. "It is too dangerous to ride, surely? There will certainly be fallen branches after a day of weather such as this!"

"Yes, Father-in-law. If you must go, at least go by carriage," Aunt Sylvia added her pleas to mine.

"Now do not fuss, I pray you. I intend to take the short-cut across the meadows and there are very few trees along that route, and now that the rain has ceased the moon will light my way."

In vain we remonstrated: the ride would do him good, he assured us: he had been housebound all day! One thing we did elicit from him: the promise that if the weather should again become wet, he would ride home in one of the Brett's carriages.

"I have ordered old Smokey to be saddled for the time when I shall be ready to set off," my grandfather said. "There is no steadier horse in the stables, as you well know, so do not fear that I shall take a toss. We two old gentlemen will amble over to Brett's Folly at a nice quiet pace and return in the same manner. Now, let us to table."

Grandpapa was proved correct in his assumption that the moon would appear and light his path, and once he had gone we settled ourselves beside a roaring fire and Mrs Ambrose read aloud to us from a most entertaining novel. We became so engrossed that we did not notice for quite some time that the poor lady was suffering from a sore throat, and when we did we were stricken with remorse.

"It is nothing, I assure you," she protested gallantly. "I should like a glass of water, that is all."

"Nonsense," my aunt said briskly. "It may be the start of a cold! Really, Mrs Ambrose, I insist that you stop this reading aloud at once. You are inflaming your throat! Come now, I think an early night is indicated, at least so far as you are concerned, with a glass of hot milk with perhaps a spoonful of brandy in it."

Mrs Ambrose still looked hesitant so I interposed:

"Yes, I think I too shall retire. Come, Mrs Ambrose, let us go up together. Carlin, time for bed. Good night, Aunt Sylvia, Uncle James, sleep well," and I led a reluctant Mrs Ambrose and an eager little dog up the stairs. Carlin knew there was always a romp in my bedchamber before we settled ourselves for the night.

"Good night, Mrs Ambrose," I said as we parted company. "Now do ring for whatever you wish. Everyone does not care for brandy as a remedy for a cold: I have heard that rum is more efficacious. Ring for whatever you desire, and I hope you pass a restful night."

She smiled. "Thank you, Miss Kimberley, for your kindness and consideration. Good night."

It was still quite early, not yet half-past nine, so my little dog and I enjoyed our game for longer than was usual. At ten o'clock I rang for Bertha to take Carlin for a short stroll whilst I made ready for bed, and then the two-hundred nightly brush-strokes of my hair must be endured. When Bertha had departed I lay snug in my bed, watching the flames flickering on the ceiling and listening to the wind howling around the house. Sleep eluded me and Carlin too was restless: he came from out of his basket and up to my bed, pleading to be allowed to curl up on the foot of it, and I had not the heart to withstand him. At last we were settled for the night: once Carlin raised his head and growled softly as a particularly strong gust of wind seemed to shake the old house to its very foundations.

"It is all right, Carlin, is is only the wind. Go to sleep, there's a good dog," I soothed, and he lowered his head upon his paws and seemed content to hear the reassurance in my voice. I had grown to love the little dog and he was devoted to me, I knew. Whenever I was in the house he was my shadow, and when I drove forth in the carriage, he would come too. The only times he could not accompany me were when I went riding: upon these occasions he would set up a lament until I bade him in a stern voice to behave himself, and then he would quieten and regard me reproachfully from his large mournful brown eyes.

Just before sleep claimed me I remember wondering whether Grandpapa had started making his way home yet from Brett's Folly. The rain had once more commenced to fall and I rather hoped he had not: if he had set out he would be caught in the downpour and soaked to the skin; whereas if he and Sir Hedworth were still discussing the merits of a bottle of brandy he would certainly return home in one of the Brett's carriages. Anyway, as he had said, he was well able to take care of himself. Although well into his sixties Grandpapa was quick of eye and firm of tread: tall and well built, he had never known a day's illness from the time I could remember. Smokey, the old grey gelding which he was riding, was sure-footed, and I doubted whether even my grandfather could coax any greater speed from him than a gentle canter! No: I was foolish to worry. All would be well: indeed, what could possibly be wrong?

From a place far away I heard an urgent voice saying:

"Wake up, Miss! Oh please wake up!" and then someone had the temerity to shake me by the shoulder! Slowly, I struggled from a deep sleep into full consciousness.

"Oh, Miss Autumn, please awaken! Oh, what is to be done?" Bertha was pulling the snug covers from about me and Carlin was barking and snarling his displeasure at this cavalier treatment.

"Bertha! Have you taken leave of your senses?" I demanded irritably. "What on earth do you think you are doing?"

"Oh Miss, I am sorry but you must awaken! Smokey has just returned to the stables in a shocking state and there is no sign of the Master! Something must be amiss!"

"What time is it?" I asked foolishly.

"It is just after midnight, Miss. Peters, the head-groom, awakened the butler, Miss, who in turn awakened me. The whole house is stirring. What's to be dono, Miss?"

"Are my aunt and uncle awake?"

"Not yet, Miss. I came to you first."

"Well, do not disturb them for a moment. Hand me my robe, I will come with you instantly."

An anxious group of people were gathered in the hall: as I descended the stairs I saw Dixon, Mrs Wilkes, Watkins and Peters together with several of the younger grooms. They all turned instinctively to me and I felt a detached calm as I asked my questions and gave my orders.

"Watkins, you are sure that Sir Mark is not in his chamber nor anywhere in the house?"

"Yes, Miss, I am sure. I was waiting up for him."

"And the horse has just come in by himself, Peters?"

"Yes, Miss, and a dreadful state he was in, too. All lathered and plastered with mud!"

"Dixon, you rouse every man-servant in the house, and you Peters do the same with the stable-men. Mrs. Wilkes, Watkins, pray assemble and make ready every available lantern and set them on the table in the main kitchen. Everyone is to gather there."

"Yes, Miss," they chorused and hurried about their various tasks.

"Bertha, come and help me to dress, and then go and clothe yourself. This is no time to be in our nightrail!"

Once we were assembled I despatched first of all a sensible looking young man for the doctor.

"He may or may not be needed, but he is to come, anyway," I said.

I then sent the younger, more agile men to cover the ground between Drawbridge Court and Brett's Folly. If my grandfather was lying injured somewhere it would be near the route of the short-cut which he had said he intended to take: the older men I directed to follow the road as far as Brett's Folly, and if they saw no sign of him before they reached our neighbour's house they were to make enquiries when they had arrived there. It was unlikely, but Grandpapa could have set out for home along the road: the state in which the horse had returned was no indication of which of the two was the right place for us to search. After the rain that had fallen during the day, the road was as likely to be nearly as miry as the fields!

"I shall accompany the younger men across country," I announced.

"Begging your pardon, Miss, but I pray that you will not!" Dixon said, apologetically. "It would be wiser for you to remain here, Miss. If you are out in the fields, there is nobody to take command, so to speak."

"Yes, Miss, I think Mr Dixon is right," interposed Mrs Wilkes.

Reluctantly I had to agree with the sense of this suggestion, and it was only after the searchers had departed that I realized nobody had thought of awakening Uncle James from his slumbers. After a little consideration I decided that it was only right he and Aunt Sylvia should be apprised of the situation, so I sent Bertha upon this errand whilst Mrs Wilkes and I gave orders to sleepy-eyed maid-servants whose curiosity at the commotion had brought them downstairs.

There was not much we could do apart from seeing that the fires were blazing in the grates: that there was a plentiful supply of hot water, and that spirits and other restoratives were close at hand. In the kitchen, refreshments and the ingredients for hot toddies were available for the searchers when they returned.

As the anxious vigil began, Aunt Sylvia and Uncle James joined me in the dining-room which gave directly onto the hall. I had left the door ajar so that the approach of anyone would instantly be heard.

"Oh, Autumn, whatever can have happened?" Aunt Sylvia looked as worried as I felt.

"Whatever it is, I am afraid that it cannot be anything good," I replied.

"I hear the horse returned in a distressed condition," Uncle James remarked. "But what was my father doing in the saddle? He promised that he would come by carriage if the rain started to fall once more, and it has now been raining for quite some time!"

"Yes, I remember hearing it start before I fell asleep," I said. "That would be about eleven o'clock: but the horse did not return until after midnight, and the ride from Brett's Folly takes no more than a quarter of an hour!"

"Unless Father-in-law has been lying injured for quite some while out in this dreadful weather, there is no accounting for the time factor," Aunt Sylvia remarked.

"But if he has been, his horse would have come

straight back to the stables long before he did," I answered. "Old Smokey knows his way home from Brett's Folly with no hand to guide him. He has made the journey often enough!"

Mrs Ambrose quietly entered the room.

"There is no news yet?" she asked. "No, that is a silly question: I can see there is not."

"Oh, Mrs Ambrose, there was no need for you to be disturbed," my aunt said. "No: there is no news, and we are all very worried. Of course, there may be a simple explanation for what has happened, but I cannot think what it could possibly be!"

"I heard an activity in the house which was most unusual for this time of night," Mrs Ambrose explained. "I saw Mrs Wilkes, and she told me what had transpired. How long have the searchers been gone?"

"Almost half-an-hour," I replied. "They have nearly had time to cover the distance between here and Brett's Folly on foot! What can they be doing?"

"My dear, it would take far longer than half-an-hour to walk to Brett's Folly on a night such as this!" Uncle James corrected me gently. "And do not forget, they are searching as they go!"

The wait seemed endless. Each one of us tried to cheer the others by saying that we thought it would all be a fuss over nothing, but as time passed we grew silent; listening for hoofbeats or the approach of someone on foot. Mercifully the rain had ceased, but the wind continued to rage and the sky was as black as pitch with no friendly star to brighten the heavens and help light the way of those who were upon this grim errand.

At last we heard the sound of horses approaching and I sprang from my seat to hurry into the hall and fling the great front door wide. Of course, it was the young groom and the doctor: I chided myself for my foolishness, it could only be they, everyone else was afoot!

"Oh Doctor Bird, so good of you to come." Uncle James had joined me in the hall. "I pray that you will forgive us for bringing you forth on a night such as this if your services are not required, but under the circumstances I think you will appreciate the situation in which we find ourselves."

"Quite so, Mr Kimberley, quite so. It is better to be safe than sorry. Fortunately I had not retired for the night when your groom arrived at my house."

The doctor was made comfortable by the fire in the dining-room, but my uncle and I remained in the hall and so were the first to hear the sound of voices; and as I looked through the window to see the flickering lanterns approach the house, I knew that our vigil would soon be over.

In silence they brought him home. My grandfather was borne upon a hurdle and in a remote way I noted that the men who carried him and others who accompanied them had taken off their greatcoats and had laid them across my Grandpapa until he was hardly visible! Yes: everyone loved him and would gladly suffer discomfort for his sake.

"Thank God you have found him!" I cried. "Is he badly hurt?" I made to lift one of the greatcoats which was covering him so snugly.

"Let be, Miss!" Somebody caught my arm. "This is no sight for your eyes!"

"Make way for the doctor!" My aunt's voice carried authority. "Doctor Bird, is it your wish that Sir Mark be carried up to his bedchamber?"

Somehow, I found myself edged away from the hurdle on which my grandfather was lying and the murmuring was so low that, strain my ears as I might, I could not hear what was said.

"Mrs Wilkes, pray lead the way to Sir Mark's bedchamber," I heard my aunt say at last, and as I made to follow she took my arm and drew me into the dining-room once more.

"Aunt Sylvia, what is amiss?" I demanded. "How badly is Grandpapa hurt? Why can I not see him?"

"It is better that you should not, Autumn," Aunt Sylvia replied gently. "Your grandfather has had an accident as we feared, but it is far worse than we dreamed possible. I am afraid that it has proved fatal!"

"Fatal? No, it is not true!" I stated flatly. "Aunt Sylvia, you must be mistaken! Grandpapa has taken a toss, that is all: he might be concussed, but it would take more than a fall on soft ground to cause serious injury! Perhaps a broken limb or maybe two, but nothing more than that, I assure you!"

Hardly pausing for breath I babbled on: refusing to accept what I had just been told: asserting and reasserting that nothing so trivial as a fall could really harm my grandfather. My words seemed to make no impression on anyone around me.

"Mrs Ambrose, will you be kind enough to stay here with Miss Kimberley whilst I go up to Sir Mark's chamber? My presence might be needed."

"Certainly. I am only too pleased to help in any way I can."

"Autumn, remain down here if you please. I shall return in a short while." Aunt Sylvia left us and I stood staring at the doorway through which she had gone.

"Miss Kimberley, pray come and sit down," Mrs Ambrose urged. "Lady Kimberley would be so relieved to see you sitting quietly when she returns to us. Compose yourself, I beg of you: we shall learn all in due course."

"Lady Kimberley? Oh, you mean my aunt! Please do not speak of her in that manner, Mrs Ambrose: to do so implies that my grandfather is dead, and that I refuse to accept. That damned fool of a doctor! How could he pronounce such a thing after just the cursory examination which he conducted in the hall, yonder? Grandpapa is lying a-swoon, that is all! As for Doctor Bird: he could not diagnose a cut finger if it was waved in front of his nose!"

What on earth could they be doing upstairs? To please Mrs Ambrose I seated myself, but I continued to talk until I found I was repeating the same words over and over again. The minutes ticked by and still I chattered: afraid that if I stopped doing so something dreadful would happen: afraid of the silence which the stilling of my voice would bring: and then afraid, just terribly, mortally afraid!

From the hall outside I began to hear the low murmur of voices: somewhere near, somebody started to sob in a high, hysterical manner, and then I heard the sound of a sharp slap, followed by silence. Then from the back of the house came a spine-chilling keening; and somewhere out in the wild, storm-ridden night a dog began to howl. It was then I knew that what Aunt Sylvia had told me was correct: the whole atmosphere of the house underwent a change. A feeling such as I had never known before overpowered me: it was fear! The howling of the wind: the wailing of a far-off voice: the melancholy lament of the dog combined with something in this very house, all added together reached the sum total of menace!

As I opened the dining-room door into the hall, so the weary older men returned accompanied by Sir Hedworth Brett. Aunt Sylvia and Uncle James were descending the stairs at about the same time, and of one accord we all returned to the dining-room.

Aunt Sylvia answered the question in my eyes: I could not bring myself to speak.

"Yes, my dear," she said. "It must have been very quick and over in a moment."

"But how?" I gasped. "What could have caused such a tragedy?"

She and Uncle James exchanged glances.

"I think it would be best if you retired to your chamber, Autumn," she suggested, quietly. "This is all so utterly distressing! Perhaps you should try to take some rest."

"What caused my grandfather's death?" I demanded. "I will know! If you will not tell me, I shall go up to Grandfather's bedchamber instantly, and find out for myself!"

I made to rise from my chair, but Uncle James held me firmly by the shoulder.

"Tell her, Sylvia," he instructed his wife. "Everyone must know, so it might as well be soon as late."

"Now, Autumn, sit quietly I pray you. Compose yourself. This is a dreadful thing which I must tell you. Oh dear, I do not think I can!"

"Then let me, Sylvia," said my uncle. "Autumn, your grandfather and my beloved sire has been most brutally murdered! He was fired upon at point-blank range by some assassin armed with a shot-gun! No: I will not spare you. You shall know all. The firearm was aimed at the side of the head with dreadful effect: as your aunt said, death must have been instantaneous!"

"Good grief, James, who could have done such a wicked, terrible thing?" Sir Hedworth gasped. "Who would wish harm upon Sir Mark Kimberley? He was loved by all, high and low!"

"God knows who has done this monstrous deed," Uncle James replied in a voice I had never heard him use before. "But as God knows, so I swear shall I! The villain will hang from the highest gallows in the land. I take a solemn oath upon it!"

Dry-eyed, I sat and gazed into the dying fire whilst the voices clamoured around me. I felt disassociated from the people occupying the same room as myself: from a far distance I seemed to hear the exclamations of horror: the ejaculations of dismay: the bitter recriminations against the lawlessness of the countryside, where nobody could go about his business in the sure belief that he would not be molested, robbed and, in a hushed voice, murdered! The anger, the grief, the strong emotions with which the room was charged seemed to wash over me: with mild surprise I discovered that I was sitting sucking my thumb as babies do, so I removed it from my mouth and still I remained silent. Suddenly I rose to my feet:

"I think I shall retire!" I calmly told the startled company. "Good night, everybody. Sleep well!"

"Are you all right, dear?" Aunt Sylvia asked. "Would you like me to come up with you to your room?"

"Yes, thank you, Aunt Sylvia, I am quite all right. There is no need for you to accompany me to my room. I shall go up alone."

"Perhaps Mrs Ambrose will be kind enough to go up with you."

"I shall go up alone! I choose to go alone!" What expression was in my eyes, upon my face, or in my voice I do not know; but whatever it was, it was sufficient for the well-wishers in the company to respect my desire for solitude.

The hall, main staircase and upstairs corridor were deserted now: I saw nobody as I made my way to my bedchamber, but as I passed my beloved grandfather's room the sounds of soft weeping could be heard through the heavy oak of the closed door. Momentarily I hesitated there, but thought better of the swift impulse which had made me pause, and continued on my way. Whoever was mourning behind that closed door was likely to be performing the last tasks upon the poor shell which only hours before was my dear, oh so very dear Grandpapa. It was not seemly that I should go in there unannounced and unexpectedly: when I saw my grandsire for the last time I wanted to look upon him when the dignity which he had borne in life was somewhat restored to him. He would wish it so.

Carlin came waddling to greet me on his little bandy legs as I entered my chamber, but even his usual exuberance was gone: with ears laid low and tail a-droop he whimpered at me, enquiringly. I picked him up and sank into an armchair, setting him upon my lap, and he and I sat gazing into the comfort of a glowing fire which Bertha had thoughtfully kept ablaze. Carlin snuggled his little body against mine and I cuddled him close. He was Grandpapa's last gift to me: the last of the many indulgences shown to me by my grandfather. I closed my eyes and re-lived in my mind the time when I was led to the study and shown the hamper containing the little dog.

They say a drowning man lives again the important moments of his life before he finally succumbs to a watery grave, and I firmly believe that this might well be so. With my mind's eye I saw my grandfather at table, telling us of the visit to London that he had planned for our enjoyment: saw him slightly embarrassed when it was discovered that he and Sir Hedworth had gone a-racing when they were supposed to be at a business meeting: saw evidence of his love for me in his every action which affected me. How he had planned for the forthcoming London season: the hiring of a house: the ordering of carriages: the engaging of a lady-companion: all, all for my benefit! I saw him astride: I saw him at table: engrossed in estate matters in his study: treading a stately measure and bowing gallantly over his partner's hand: performing a hundred everyday actions; alas, to do so no more!

We sat until the dawn was breaking, Carlin and I: we sat until I had almost convinced myself that this must be a ghastly nightmare which had come to disturb my slumbers: yes, nearly convinced myself but at the back of my mind I knew that this was not so. My grandfather was the rock upon which I had built my life: he was the shield against the outside world! Strong, tender, loving and wise; steadfast in adversity, generous to a fault, from my infancy I had regarded him as a god-like figure, totally indestructible; and now, with no warning, no presentment of doom, he was gone!

FIVE

THAT anyone so deeply loved and highly respected as my grandfather had been to meet with such a senseless violent death was harrowing enough, but to make matters worse if that were possible, was the fact that some time must elapse before he could decently be laid to rest. My uncle, now Sir James, proved an unexpected tower of strength. He and Sir Hedworth Brett spared we ladies of the household all they could, but some unpleasant interviews had to be faced: there were questions without number to be answered: the dreadful night to be lived through again, and again, and yet again!

Of course there must be a post-mortem, then an inquest at which the only verdict could be murder by person or persons unknown. The police were everywhere: questioning the maid-servants until they became hysterical: cross-examining the men-servants, most of whom would willingly have risked all to serve anyone bearing the name of Kimberley! Newspaper reporters lay in wait for anyone leaving the house until we were afraid to set foot out of doors.

For all the questioning: for all the searching for clues as to the identity of the assassin: the turmoil, the indignities suffered, the grief which was intensified a hundred-fold were all for nothing! All that was established was the fact that my grandfather had been about to ride through an open gate from one meadow into another. It was assumed from the position in which his poor body had fallen that the fatal shot had been fired by someone standing beside the gatepost in the shelter of the hedge which separated the two meadows.

The mystery remained: for days, weeks after the terrible tragedy we talked of little else when we were alone. At table, in the evenings, we kept coming back to the subject which was uppermost in our minds. After a great deal of reflection, I strongly held the view that the dreadful deed had been an accident: certainly no less terrible in the result, but an accident nonetheless.

"Grandpapa was loved and respected by all," I said. "Nobody bore him any ill-will: he was fair and just and generous, so it could not have been anybody with a grudge! If he had been on the road I would have suspected footpads, but he was not! No robber would wait on a stormy night at a gate between two meadows on the chance that some wayfarer might come a-riding by: the thought is too ridiculous to even be considered!"

"How came anybody to be in the shadow of that hedge at all?" Aunt Sylvia demurred.

"Poaching!" I asserted. "I am convinced that Grandpapa startled somebody who had no business to be there, and the gun went off accidentally."

"But my dear, no poacher would venture forth on a night such as that one," Uncle James interposed. "It was so dark a man could not see a hand in front of his face!"

"Ah, but it was not so when Grandpapa started riding home, otherwise he would have come home in a carriage. Sir Hedworth had told us that although the wind was rough, the moon was trying to make its way through the clouds when Grandpapa left Brett's Folly. It became so much darker when the rain started to fall again, later on."

"Mrs Ambrose, you are silent! What do you think?" asked my aunt.

"Well, I did not like to venture an opinion unless expressly asked," she replied. "But all things considered, I find I am inclined to agree with Miss Kimberley. Sir Mark was not robbed and as Miss Kimberley says, no foot-pad would lie in wait at that remote spot. It was not done for the sake of malice, we are agreed upon that. Apart from the immediate family and perhaps a few minor beneficiaries nobody stands to gain from Sir Mark's sudden demise, so what other explanation is there? Yes, a poacher: caught unawares, startled out of all reason, who discharged his weapon accidentally and then panicked and ran for his life!"

"Leaving my poor grandfather lying in the mud with his dear head——." I buried my face in my hands, then my aunt's arm was about my shoulders and she said quietly:

"S-sh, Autumn, do not think of it. It is pointless to go over it all again and again. Let us speak of something else."

"No, Aunt Sylvia, if we speak of something else we shall still be thinking of Grandpapa. Oh, if only there was something we could do! I know we cannot bring him back, but I should like to know who was responsible for my grandsire's untimely end."

"But there is nothing to help us find out," Uncle James reminded me. "The police are baffled: any footprint which might have led us to the villain was obliterated by our own men. In their haste to bring their master home, they had no thought for preserving any possible clues!"

As time passed we picked up the threads of our everyday lives, and although the bereavement we had suffered was still ever present in our minds, gradually the pain softened a little. Life must go on, and there were busy times ahead for us all.

Even though I had known I was my grandfather's heir, I had no exact knowledge of how he would bestow his estate when the time came, which unfortunately was now; but when Grandpapa's Will was read to us it contained no surprises. At the age of twenty-one I should inherit most of the land, property and fortune. Until then, some eighteen months distant, the estate would be administered jointly by my uncle, now Sir James Kimberley, and Mr Dawson, the solicitor: also Uncle James and Aunt Sylvia were to be my legal guardians until my majority was reached. Years ago Grandpapa had settled a comfortable sum upon Uncle James, and now he would enjoy an additional income from certain properties not willed to me directly, but as my uncle and aunt were childless, this last-mentioned portion of the estate would revert to me in due course: I prayed many years hence. There were favourite charities which would receive handsome amounts: there were keepsakes for friends: Grandpapa's senior servitors had all been remembered, and the Vicar of St Paul's could have the new organ for his church which he so earnestly desired.

"Mr Dawson, there has been no firm agreement regarding the hiring of the house in London, has there?" Uncle James asked the solicitor.

"No, Sir James, nothing has been finally settled. There will be no difficulty on that score."

It seemed so strange to hear my aunt and uncle addressed as Sir James and Lady Kimberley. It was sad, too, to reflect upon the fact that with the passing of my uncle, the name of Kimberley would also die. Of course, if Perry should wed Lady Isobel I would remain a spinster for the rest of my days, I was resolved upon that issue: but when my days upon this earth were ended, there would be no more Kimberleys to dwell in their ancient home at Drawbridge Court!

Of course there would be no London season this year: nor, if I had my way, in any future year. The tight-lacing and daily parades to improve my deportment were all for nothing: but how gladly I would have suffered them if they could have brought back the happy carefree days on which they had taken place. How light-heartedly we had welcomed the future: the only cloud upon my horizon had been Lady Isobel Frost, but although I knew she was still there to threaten my hopes and dreams of romance, her presence had paled into the veriest insignificance after I had found myself, for the first time in my life, face to face with grief and tragedy.

* * *

Mrs Ambrose was a treasure in the weeks that followed. Mr Dawson took himself back to London and, although he and Uncle James were to administer the estate until I came of age, I found that the day-to-day affairs of Drawbridge Court and the lands around it fell squarely on my shoulders. After the first few occasions when my uncle had sent Mr Biggs, the estate agent, to me for permission to carry out needed repairs on this farm building or that, the agent came to me directly without approaching Uncle James at all!

"Miss Kimberley, Farmer Ashley is clamouring for a new roof for that barn of his! What am I to tell him?"

"You may tell him, Mr Biggs, that you and I will inspect it together tomorrow morning. If we agree that it needs attention, attended to it shall be!"

"And there's that matter of the tenancy being renewed at Clover Farm, Miss. The tenant up and died last Michaelmas, and there is only the widow and one son there now."

"Do they wish for the tenancy to be renewed in their name then, Mr Biggs?" I asked.

"Yes, Miss, they do, but I'm against it."

"Why so, Mr Biggs?"

"The son is a shiftless good-for-nothing, Miss, and the widow is not one of these capable bodies who can manage without a trustworthy man to see to things."

"I shall consider the matter, Mr Biggs. Will that be all for today?"

"Yes, Miss. At what time shall we ride over to Farmer Ashley's place tomorrow?"

"Be at the stables around ten o'clock if you please. Good morning, Mr Biggs, I shall see you tomorrow at that time."

These were just two examples of the decisions I had to make, then there were the household accounts to be inspected and daily orders to be given to Dixon and Mrs Wilkes. I must visit the stables regularly, for although I knew Peters the head-groom would not tolerate any slip-shod work from his underlings, it was my place as mistress to approve and pass remark so that he should know that his efforts did not go unnoticed.

For the first time in years I descended to the cellars with Dixon. There I must dole out to him the wines to be consumed by the household, and he must enter them into his cellar-book so that a strict accounting could be kept. I had suggested that this was most unnecessary: I knew Dixon was no secret toper, nor was he even capable of any act of dishonesty; but he looked so pained when I proffered the keys to him that I had not insisted that he should take them.

"Oh, no, Miss, it would not be right! It is always

done thus, in every household in the land it is done so!"

"Very well, Dixon, but you must advise me. I know nothing of wines so you must tell me how I should go on: what will be needed, and when I must order more."

"Certainly, Miss, I shall be pleased to. But you must keep the keys in your own hand!"

The wine cellars lay under the main front of the house: under the kitchens in the east wing lay the fuel cellars, and beneath the west wing were the cellars which Uncle James had converted into a laboratory. What he did in them was a mystery: he spent the better part of every day down there, usually just emerging for meals, but there were occasions when he was not even to be seen at table!

"Uncle James, what can you find to occupy you for such a great length of time?" I asked him one evening.

"Ah, Autumn, if you were endowed with an interest in science you would not ask me that," he replied with a gentle smile. "This is a marvellous age in which we live. All over the world men are discovering new wonders. Take the railways for an instance, and the great engineering feats which are taking place so frequently: they are all miracles of man's ingenuity. At last he had seen a way of harnessing the mighty powers of nature, and of making them work to his will!"

"Yes, Uncle James, I know, but not in the cellars of Drawbridge Court, surely?"

"You may smile and you may tease, little niece, but I know what I know! And I will let you into a secret: one day, not in the too distant future, I may surprise you! How would you like a famous uncle, eh? One whose name might be found written in the pages of history in years to come?"

"What do you mean, James?" Aunt Sylvia was startled into asking.

"I mean, my love, that my time has not been completely wasted. I am not sure, but I might, just might, mind you, have discovered something which will set the scientific world by the ears!" He looked quite smug as he replied.

"Oh, Sir James, how exciting!" Mrs Ambrose exclaimed. "Can you tell us what it is? In a simple way of course, so that we might understand?"

"No, dear lady, I will say no more! Until my work is complete, my lips are sealed!"

"You call me a tease, Uncle James," I chided him. "You, sir, I find positively aggravating! Come now, you can give us a hint, surely?"

"Not a word! No: you together with the rest of the world will learn all in due course. Oh, that reminds me, ladies, I must go up to London for a few days next week. There is to be a meeting at the Royal Society which I wish to attend, and there is a little research which I can undertake at the same time."

"But James, you have not left this house in years!" Aunt Sylvia said. "Must you go?"

"Indeed I must. There has been nothing to tempt me from this house, as you say, in years; but now that my experiments are nearing completion I find I must refer to more specialized knowledge than that which is available to me here. This meeting, too, might be of vital importance. I shall be gone for perhaps three days, certainly no longer."

I was pleased that Watkins, my grandfather's valet, had now become manservant to my uncle: until lately, Uncle James had never thought he needed a valet, but it would be unthinkable for the now Sir

James Kimberley to go haring off to London without his own man! Of one thing I could be sure; Watkins, in a truly deferential way, would see that my uncle did not bring shame to the name of Kimberley by appearing in public in his bedroom slippers, or by sitting down to dine clad in morning attire.

Now that we had overcome our initial amazement at Uncle James' startling news, we were all eager to see him set off for the capital. Oh, how wonderful it would be if he had really discovered something important! After all these years of work: bearing with if not near contempt, at least condescending smiles at his obsession with scientific matters; how utterly fantastic it would be if Uncle James could show to an astonished world that he was no fool, but a great man! Yes: I was guilty together with the rest of the household of thinking that nothing would ever come of these endless experiments taking place in the cellars, but how proud we should be if we were proved wrong! And Grandpapa, how justly proud he would have been to have sired a son who might bring benefit to the whole of mankind! Oh, if only he were here now!

* * *

From the time of my earliest recollections, Uncle James had been a shadowy figure with no real importance in my life: oh, I loved him dearly and I had never known him anything but kind and gentle in an absentminded way, but I could not recall him ever asserting an opinion over any matter of importance until Grandfather's recent death. Now that we had recovered somewhat from the shock and grief of our bereavement, Uncle James had reverted to his normal ways, just appearing for meals, if at all; but Drawbridge Court seemed surprisingly different once he had departed for London, taking Watkins with him. Upon reflection I decided that the reason for this must be that there was no gentleman in the house for the first time that I could remember.

The month of April is, I think, the loveliest in the year, with the promise of summer lying ahead, and everything fresh and burgeoning with life. Upon the day after that on which Uncle James had set off for London, my aunt persuaded me to take a turn about the gardens with her.

"Come, Autumn, set your duties aside for just this once," she coaxed. "After all, there is nothing which needs your attention that will not wait!"

I did not need a great deal of cajoling: the bright sunshine streaming through the windows added to the temptation to play truant.

"Where is Mrs Ambrose?" I asked.

"In her room, I believe. Come, let us slip out before she rejoins us. Oh, I do not mean to be unkind and I am very fond of the lady, but it would be nice to take a stroll, just you and I, with no outsider present."

"Very well. I must fetch a bonnet and shawl first though. You wait here and I will not be long," I agreed.

With Carlin at my heels I ascended the stairs and trod quietly along the corridor above until I reached my bedchamber. It was extremely foolish of me I know, but although the thick pile of the carpet made the necessity for creeping needless, nonetheless I opened the door of my chamber as noiselessly as possible. Yes: it would be pleasant to enjoy the spring sunshine with just my aunt for company, and if Mrs Ambrose appeared before we had left the house, good manners would force us to invite her to join us. Stealthily I opened the wardrobe door so that I should not disturb her as she busied herself in the chamber next to mine, but I had forgotten Carlin. Bonnets and shawls meant outings so far as he was concerned, and he whowed his approval of this imminent treat by racing wildly around my bedchamber, barking like a mad thing as he did so.

"S-sh, Carlin! Be quiet you naughty dog," I hissed to no avail, and I fully expected Mrs Ambrose to be at her door as I emerged with Carlin from mine. But no: fortune was with us, and like a child escaping from the schoolroom I took to my heels and fled along the corridor and down the stairs, with Carlin in hot pursuit.

"Take my arm, " I invited Aunt Sylvia as we left the house.

"Yes, I shall be pleased to do so, my dear," she answered. "No, do not look so concerned. I can see quite well really, but it is pleasantly companionable to walk together like this. I know I am becoming very short-sighted: distances defeat me completely, but things which are close I can see really well, especially on such a bright day as this!"

"Let us go down to the lake," I suggested. "The daffodils surrounding it are in full flower, and every time I look at them their sheer beauty takes my breath away!"

We followed the little stream down to the water's edge and stood in silence, drinking in the wonder of the glorious scene spread like a tapestry before our enchanted eyes. A tapestry of green, gold and silver: the silver of the lake, the gold of the daffodils, the fresh greensward all set against nature's backcloth of yet more silver; that of the birch trees which in a short month from now would set off to equal perfection the azure of bluebells.

"Oh, Autumn, how fortunate we are to be able to

stroll from our home and within minutes see sights such as this!" Aunt Sylvia sighed. "How I pity all those poor exiles in foreign lands who can never see the magic of an English spring. Let us linger here awhile. I wish to capture this moment, so that whenever I close my eyes I can call this scene to mind."

We stood and listened to the lapping of the wavelets as a gentle breeze ruffled the lake and rustled the branches of the trees, sending the golden trumpets of the daffodils swaying, and in this quiet moment a great feeling of melancholy overtook me.

"Oh, Aunt Sylvia, why is life so sad? It is so very beautiful, but sad as well. Time passes so swiftly: today we stand revelling in the loveliness of the world around us, but even in a few short weeks from now, it will all be changed. Yes, I know there is always something to replace that which has gone before. Bluebells will replace these daffodils, and when they too are gone the roses will flower; but at times like this I am frightened. It is all so relentless: nobody can still the passage of time, I know, but why does it have to pass so quickly?"

"Autumn, dear, you should not allow your emotions to overset you. We have stood here long enough: let us resume our stroll. At your age time should not be a matter for deep consideration: as one becomes older it begins to assume a more important role in one's life. Ah me, when I was nineteen, time did not worry me: in those days I thought it would be impossible for me to grow old: it was a thing which would happen to others, but never to me! Now I know better. Here am I; fair, fat and forty, as the saying goes. Yes, my love; as Lady Kimberley I am fair, fat and forty, but the Miss Sylvia Everrett of twenty-odd years ago was a fairy sprite who was ageless! That was how I thought of myself in those days, and it is how you should regard your own image. The nineteen-year-old Miss Autumn Kimberley is eternal: it is only a possible Lady Someone-else who could ever become old!"

As we sauntered back to the house we were chuckling at preposterous visions of me twenty years hence and continuing our nonsensical conversation as we went. My fit of gloom had left me completely, and as we skirted the house so that we might approach the front door I noticed one of the french windows in the library was open.

"Ah, that will save us from walking around the front of the house!" I remarked. "Someone has been thoughtful enough to leave one of the library windows open. Let us enter that way."

I preceded my aunt so that I might help her over the shallow step when suddenly Carlin emitted such a furious spate of barking that I nearly jumped out of my skin. Involuntarily, I glanced up, and just had time to grasp my aunt and hurl us both sideways before one of the great twisted chimneys crashed to the ground, falling on the exact spot on which I had been standing a split second earlier.

"God in Heaven, what was that?" gasped Aunt Sylvia as momentarily I lay stupefied by the shock of what had just taken place. "Autumn, are you all right?"

"Yes, Aunt, I think so," I replied shakily. "We have just missed death by inches, you and I. Let me help you to rise."

There was the sound of running feet and soon a crowd of servants was clustering about us. We all stood staring at the remains of the great chimney which had adorned the roof since I do not know when, then presently I allowed myself to be led into the house and given strong tea to still the tremors in my still shaking limbs. When I had recovered my equilibrium a little I realized that my dog was not with me.

"Carlin!" I exclaimed. "Where is he? Oh, Aunt Sylvia, he saved us both. Say he is not hurt, I beg you!"

"I do not know, my dear. In all this flurry I had not thought of him. Mrs Wilkes, send someone to find him if you please."

"I will go and seek him," offered Mrs Ambrose.

But now that I was in command of my limbs again I could not wait for information from someone else!

"No, it is all right. I must find him. Pray God he is not harmed!" I replied, and returned to where the remnants of the chimney lay outside the library window.

The little dog did not take much finding, and I breathed a prayer of gratitude when I saw him standing as jaunty as ever in almost the same position as he had been a few minutes earlier. There were menservants and gardeners standing amongst the debris, scratching their heads and speculating on the cause of the near disaster; but the little creature that was responsible for my aunt's and my safety was completely ignored. He was still staring up at the rooftop from where the chimney had fallen: as he saw me he whimpered and wagged his tail, but he remained staring upwards, occasionally uttering a soft growl.

"Come, Carlin!" For a treat I picked him up and cuddled him close and he snuggled against my shoulder, but as we entered the house he continued to crane his neck: no doubt to see if more exciting things were about to descend from the heavens, and the low growl which I heard was perhaps one of disappointment that the diversion was over!

Although not badly hurt I was still considerably shaken, and when Aunt Sylvia expressed a desire to seek the solitude of her chamber and suggested that I should retire to mine for an hour or so, I did not demur. Once there, I was able to inspect my injuries which amounted to a badly grazed elbow and a bruise upon my knee which was already beginning to assume an assortment of hues, and promised more colour to come as time progressed. Bertha bathed and dressed my wounds, and then I put on a *peignoir* so that I might relax in comfort: but no sooner was I settled than there came a gentle tap upon my door and Aunt Sylvia entered, similarly clad.

"I thought you intended to lie down for a short while," I said in surprise.

"Yes, dear. I will anon. I just came to see how you were before I did so."

"I am a trifle bruised, that is all. How did you fare in our narrow escape?"

"No worse than you did, I am thankful to say. Oh, my dear, how fortunate we were! It is all thanks to Carlin, and you of course! Your prompt action saved my life, and I have not yet thanked you: and if it had not been for your dog giving warning as he did of the peril we were in, we should certainly have perished!"

"You are a very clever dog, Carlin," I agreed, and he, fully aware of our approbation, lay on his back with paws aloft waiting to be made much of.

"Well, if you are sure you are all right I shall retire to my chamber," Aunt Sylvia announced. "I will come down for dinner, but do not look for me before then. I think I shall take one of my drops."

"Yes, Aunt, you do that. I shall see you later."

My brain was too active for me to sleep, so in an hour or so I made my toilette and descended the stairs. Dixon was in the hall, and I bade him attend me in the dining-room where the fire was blazing cosily.

"Has the debris of the fallen chimney been cleared away, Dixon?" I asked.

"Yes, Miss, it was seen to immediately afterwards. May I say, Miss, how thankful I am that you and Lady Kimberley were not badly hurt, or even worse!"

"Thank you, Dixon. Needless to say, we too are most thankful. Now, first thing in the morning I wish for a sensible man to go up on the roof, and make a thorough inspection: you will arrange it if you please. He is to examine the tiles and pay particular attention to the chimney-stacks, the chimneys themselves, the coping, guttering: in short, I want the whole of the roof to be given a complete scrutiny. I quite realize that it should have been done before this: Drawbridge Court is a very old house and I cannot remember when last the roof was examined."

"Begging your pardon, Miss, but Sir Mark had all that seen to not five years ago!"

"Well, the narrow escape my aunt and I had this afternoon tells me that it should be done frequently. I do not want any more near disasters to take place here! We have experienced some very rough weather, particularly during this last month or so, and I suppose that an old house such as this cannot be expected to withstand the elements without weakening at some point or another."

"Very well, Miss, I shall see that your instructions are carried out."

"You may tell the man selected for the task, that for any serious fault he finds aloft; such as a crack in a chimney or anything which might create a hazard, he will receive a guinea!"

"I do not think that will be necessary, Miss," Dixon demurred. "The work will be well done, I assure you."

"There are no doubts in my mind upon that score," I smiled. "But although the task will not be dangerous, it is not one which I would readily undertake! The roof is surrounded by a narrow walk I know, so that the gutters may easily be cleared; but some parts of the roof may be difficult to inspect. Anyway, I will stand by what I have said: a guinea for every serious fault found!"

The evening passed pleasantly enough: neither Aunt Sylvia nor I had received any great hurt from the accident, but as dinner was served we seemed to talk of nothing else until I was weary of the subject.

"I can still hear that dreadful crash ringing in my ears," Mrs Ambrose said. "I had seen you two ladies down by the lake from my window, and I made haste to join you. But by the time I had donned bonnet and cloak and reached the spot where you had been standing, you must have been making your way back to the house. In any event, you were gone; and as I retraced my steps I heard that terrible crash when the chimney fell. What a blessing that neither of you were hurt!"

"Oh, Mrs Ambrose, I feel quite faint at the thought of what might have been," replied my aunt.

"Then pray think of something else," I suggested, firmly. "Something pleasant. For instance, I wonder how Uncle James is enjoying his visit to London?"

This happy thought of mine led the conversation away from chimney-pots and sudden catastrophe; Mrs Ambrose was swift to take my hint: she really is the most amusing creature! In seemingly no time at all she had us laughing at some of the most absurd inventions which she would beg Uncle James to set his mind to, upon his return from London.

* * *

Grandpapa's study I had adopted as my own

domain. Here it was that I could be found most mornings, studying the household accounts or conducting the business of the estate: I had also made it known that at this time of day I was available if any lesser member of the staff wished to bring a grievance to my ears, or consult me upon a personal problem.

I was engrossed in my tasks when Dixon came to me next morning, and I glanced up at him enquiringly.

"It is the matter of the roof, Miss. I must speak to you about it without delay."

"Why, Dixon? Have you experienced any difficulty in finding a man to go up there?" I asked.

"No, Miss, young Jed Simpson has undertaken the task. He is a steady lad, quite reliable; with sharp eyesight and and a good head for heights."

"Then what is the problem, Dixon?"

"I should like you to come up and see for yourself, Miss. As you know, you may gain access to the roof through one of the lumber-room windows: from there you can step directly out on to that narrow walk which surrounds the roof, just inside the guttering. Well, Miss, Jed did just that. He stepped from the window on to the walk, and then he noticed that someone had been there before him! There were footprints, Miss! A man's footprints in the dirt, leading away from and returning to the window, and clear to see, as though they were only made recently!"

"Are you sure, Dixon? Could they not have belonged to Jed Simpson?"

"No, Miss. Jed's footprints had covered some of these others for the first yard or so, but as soon as he noticed them he came back into the house and reported to me. Anyway, Miss, these other footprints are quite different from those made by Jed!"

"I will come up with you at once, Dixon. Will I have to go out on the roof?"

"No, Miss. You may see all quite distinctly from the window in the lumber-room."

In silence we made our way up to the room which gave access to the roof, there to find a troubled looking Jed.

"There, Miss! Just you take a look at that!" invited Dixon, and I gazed in bewilderment at the narrow walk, where plainly to be seen were two sets of footprints in the grime. One set stopped short about two yards from where they had started: these were large, studded, and deeper than the others. The second set were those of a smaller, lighter man: a man who had left behind him the impression that he was not afraid of heights if the distance between one footprint and the next was any criterion: a man whose stride had carried him swiftly along the walk and back again; but to where, and for what purpose?

"Jed, would you mind following these footprints to see where they lead?" I asked the young man.

"It will be a pleasure, Miss," he replied cheerfully, and Dixon and I watched him clamber through the window to tread carefully in the wake of one who had gone before, until he disappeared from view around a corner. In only a few short minutes Jed was safely back inside the house; and although as I had stood there awaiting his return my mind had rejected as impossible the thought that anything evil was in our midst, I was not really surprised when he told his tale.

"You'll never guess where they lead to, Miss!" he said in a shocked voice.

"Then pray tell us, Jed," I replied calmly.

"Speak up, man. Do not keep your betters waiting," interposed Dixon, helpfully.

"Sorry, Miss. Straight to that there chimney-stack, they lead, Miss. You know, the one from where that chimney tumbled, yesterday!"

"They went no further, Jed?" I questioned, hopefully. But I knew what his answer would be before he had time to utter it.

"No, Miss. I followed them most careful-like. Up to that there chimney-stack they went, then they were mussed up a bit around it, and then they came straight back to this here window!"

"There was nothing else to be seen?" I asked. "Nothing which might indicate who has been up here?"

Jed stared at me blankly.

"Was there anything else on the roof which was unusual, Jed?" Dixon questioned. "A piece of paper or a handkerchief? Anything at all?"

"Oh, I see what you mean. No sir, no Miss, nothing but muck and leaves and such."

"Very well, Jed, thank you," I said. "Now you continue your inspection of the roof: you have already earned one guinea, and if you come across anything else of importance there will be more. One thing, though. I do not wish for you to mention these footprints to anyone else. Do you understand, Jed?"

From his puzzled look I could see that he did not, but he answered stoutly enough:

"Yes, Miss. Anything you say, Miss," and with that I had to be content.

Dixon and I returned to the study and waited for each other to speak.

"Well, Dixon, what do you think?" I asked at last.

"I do not know, Miss. The only thing of which I can think, I hesitate to put into words!"

"We might as well face it, Dixon. You and I are both wondering if someone caused that chimney to fall in hope that I, my aunt, or both of us would either be injured or killed outright!" I said, baldly.

"It cannot be so, Miss. For what reason would anyone do such a thing? Who would rejoice or benefit if you or Lady Kimberley were maimed, or met with a sudden end? There is nobody!"

"Nobody in his right mind," I answered, slowly. "But what if we are dealing with someone to whom a sense of reason does not apply?"

"But who, Miss? There is nobody of unsound mind in this house!"

"Not to our knowledge, Dixon, but it could be anyone! There is a large staff in this household: it could be any one of them, or even someone from outside Drawbridge Court altogether! As my aunt and I returned yesterday, a french window in the library was ajar: anyone could have entered the house through there, or through any one of a dozen other doors and windows!"

"Oh, Miss, what are we to do? If a lunatic is at large, I must instruct the staff to secure all doors and windows until he is caught!"

"But what if he is already inside the house, Dixon?" I asked. "What then?"

"Well, I could narrow it down by measuring those footprints on the roof, Miss, and desiring all the menservants to compare their feet with those! We know he is not very large, so I would only need to compare the foot-size of the medium-sized and smaller servants."

"And what explanation could we give them for this unusual exercise?" Even in the light of this serious situation, I could not refrain from smiling. But the enterprising Dixon was equal to the challenge.

"New boots, Miss!" he replied with aplomb. "I am

afraid it will be rather costly, Miss, but I do think it is worth it for the sake of our peace of mind!"

"Then you must measure the feet of all the men, Dixon. We cannot have it said that men with large feet are penalized at Drawbridge Court!"

"Very well, Miss. I shall see to it without delay."

"This is something like a macabre version of the story of Cinderella!" I remarked.

"I cannot think of any other way to set about the task, Miss," Dixon confessed.

"No: neither can I!" Suddenly I laughed. "Do you know, Dixon, you and I have been thinking of terrible things, when the explanation could be quite simple! The oldest of human faults: nothing more or less than common curiosity! What if one of our most trustworthy servants had the same dreadful suspicions as we, and went up there to investigate with only my welfare at heart? The whole thing might well have been an accident, and whoever went up there to see for himself how it came about, did not even think of the footprints he himself would leave behind, and which would look so suspicious!"

"Well, that could be the answer, Miss." Dixon still sounded doubtful.

"Of course it is! Oh, the men can have their new boots, if it will set your mind at rest. But I think we shall find I am right!"

And so it was resolved: Jed found one or two loose tiles, but that was all: Dixon's Cinderella theory came to nothing, because any one of a number of smaller menservants or lads who had access to the house, could have been responsible for the mysterious footprints; and although there was a great deal of speculation and wonder that all the menservants should have new boots for no apparent purpose, I found that the pounds were well spent if for no other reason that I was able to chuckle myself to sleep for nights to come, at the thought of the ridiculous suspicions which Dixon and I had briefly held!

SIX

UNCLE JAMES arrived home two days later, and although apart from the incident of the fallen chimney-pot nothing in our day-to-day lives had differed during his absence, at his return the whole house seemed to take on a more solid and comfortable atmosphere. It was strange, I thought, that Uncle James might bury himself in his work for days at a time, be extremely absent-minded when he did put in an appearance: be considered vague, and a trifle divorced from reality; but to know that he was here, within call, made all the difference in the world to me!

We were agog to hear his news, and he told us a little of what he thought would interest us.

"I must go up to town more often," he announced. "It is only now that I realize how out of touch I have become during these last years. No, ladies, I did not indulge in any gaiety whilst I was in London: but I met so many interesting people that the visit was all that I could have wished!"

"And your research, Uncle James?" I asked. "You were able to conduct it satisfactorily?"

"Yes, my dear, most successfully. Some of the gentlemen whom I met were most helpful, and gratifyingly interested in what I had to tell them."

"And yet you cannot tell us!" Aunt Sylvia sounded a little hurt.

"Not yet, my love, but I will soon. Very soon!"

As we sat in the drawing-room I reflected that it

was strange that one could live with a fellow being for all of one's life, and yet not know them! Uncle James had always been regarded as a slightly helpless figure for the rest of the world to smile at: now, here before my very eyes, he was changing into a different person altogether. Changing? Nay: I should say he had changed! His manner was more direct: his speech was more decisive: he seemed very well aware of what was taking place around him, and he even appeared to have grown a little in stature! But had he changed at all, or were we seeing for the first time the Uncle James who only came to life behind the closed door of his laboratory? No muddleheaded simpleton could achieve great things in the field of science, I knew; and therefore I marvelled! But at the same time, I felt a trifle uneasy!

* * *

The Bretts were invited to dine with us on the approaching Saturday. Although we were still in deep mourning for Grandpapa, and would be for a long while to come, this could not be regarded as unseemly entertaining! The news that Perry would drive over with them and beg his dinner from us was the happiest I had heard in a long time, and to even our numbers at table I suggested that we invite the vicar as well: he was a pleasant person with no wife with whom we must contend; and although his housekeeper looked to his needs well enough, I knew that he thoroughly enjoyed a meal where the company and conversation would be as agreeable as the dishes served.

Before I descended the stairs to join the others ere our guests arrived, I found myself staring at my reflection in the dressing chest mirror. My face looked unusually pale against my sombre gown. I sighed: only last September I had yearned to be allowed to wear black and now my wish was granted, but at what cost! My aunt and I both wore similar gowns for day and evening: black, with white lawn collars and cuffs. Aunt Sylvia occasionally allowed herself the frivolity of a pair of jet earrings, but I had no heart for jewellery of any sort. Mrs Ambrose did not wear deep mourning as did we others, but although I do not think that she possessed any garment in what could be described as a bright colour, I had noticed that since my grandfather's death she had laid aside the pale blues and greens which she had favoured until then, and now wore greys, fawns, and similar quiet hues. It was in keeping with the rest of her character that although not in mourning herself she should have regard for the feelings of others, and I was not ungrateful for her thoughtfulness towards us.

The evening was most convivial in a quiet way: when the gentlemen joined us in the drawing-room after the meal and I was presiding over the tea-tray, the talk turned quite naturally to local affairs. Of course, the news of the near catastrophe at Drawbridge Court had been on everyone's lips: it was the most interesting, and had caught the attention of our neighbours for miles around.

"I cannot describe my feelings when I heard of your narrow escape," Lady Mary said. "Your good angel must have been very near that day! Just think, if you, Autumn, had not had the presence of mind to fling your aunt and yourself clear of that great chimney, we might not be sitting here now. Oh, I shudder to even think of it!"

"Actually, it was my little dog that saved our lives," I replied. "He was more alert than I, and his bark gave me warning of what was about to happen."

"Well, my niece has made sure that nothing else will fall from the roof," said Uncle James. "During my absence she has had a thorough inspection made, and has even set things in train for the damage to be repaired!"

"And such a business it is, too!" I remarked. "First of all I had Mr Biggs assess the extent of the damage, and then a builder must come from Rochester to see what he thinks, as well. The upshot of it all is that a new chimney must be made especially, to be in keeping with the rest of those on the chimney-stack. How long this will take I do not know, and neither it seems does anyone else: and then we must have scaffolding set against the west wing so that the chimney can be put in place when the time comes. If the business is finished before high summer I shall be much surprised!"

"What a very capable young lady you are, Autumn!" exclaimed Sir Hedworth. "Most gently nurtured females would have swooned away, and left all to others: it is most refreshing to hear of such decisive action on the part of a young lady not long out of the schoolroom!"

These kind words which were said with such approval only served to make me aware of the impression I must have given to my interested audience, one of whom was Perry. Capable, decisive of action, these were the adjectives applied to me, whereas I wanted to be thought of as gentle and feminine! It was common knowledge that whilst a gentleman might admire authoritative traits in some women, he would not want them in his wife! Lady Isobel Frost could never be accused of such sensible behaviour: she would flutter her eyelashes helplessly, and a score of gentlemen would rush to her aid.

To deny these attributes of Sir Hedworth, I replied quickly:

"Oh, no sir, I took no great part in all this. Uncle James was absent, and so I left the matter in the hands of my agent, Mr Biggs. He it was who saw to all these things, and then reported the results of his labours to me."

"Now, my dear, do not disclaim!" Aunt Sylvia nearly spoiled all. "I was extremely proud of the way you handled everything!"

"Well, you will not think so when you hear what I have to say now," I replied. "Only Dixon and I know of this, but now I feel I must share the jest with you all. I find it so amusing that I think it would be mean not to allow you to smile at my folly."

And so I told the assembled company of how the strange footprints had been found upon the roof: and of how Dixon and I had immediately leapt to the conclusion that a madman was in our midst, or at least had access to the house. I built up my story to make it as entertaining as possible, and I can truly say that I had the undivided attention of everyone present. Dixon's excellent notion of measuring the feet of the men-servants to see whose would fit into the mysterious footprints was met with by murmurs of approval: but when I came to the end of my tale, and told of how any number of men in the household could have been the culprit, and that I now firmly believed that there was nothing more sinister than common curiosity in the house, there was a general release of mirth from my audience.

"So every manservant has a new pair of boots!" I concluded. "This has cost quite a few pounds, and is the price which I must pay for indulging in needless suspicion. But I beg you all, do not make this tale common property, or I shall be the laughing stock of the county!"

Perry seemed the most amused by this foolish story which I had told against myself. Long after the rest of the company started discussing other matters, he came and sat beside me and quizzed me about household concerns, stroking Carlin as he did so, to the little dog's great delight.

"Well, this small animal has earned his keep if he never does another worthy deed in his life!" Perry said.

"Yes, he is my shadow, and tiny as he is, he guards me well!"

* * *

The summer which lay ahead would be spent very quietly: there was no question of us accepting, or even of receiving invitations to the various rural pleasures with which we country folk entertained ourselves. Everyone knew we were in mourning and had crossed us off their lists, temporarily: apart from our visits to church, and the occasional small dinner party with our closest friends, we at Drawbridge Court must be content with our own company until the period of our mourning was over.

Even now Grandpapa was gone from us, I still had reason to bless him every day: he had thought to give me Carlin, and he too had been responsible for Mrs Ambrose making her home with us. This lady had taken a great burden off my shoulders: oh, I do not mean an unpleasant one, but she kept my aunt amused and occupied, leaving me free to carry out my duties with an easy conscience. The days passed swiftly enough for me: indeed, some of them were not long enough in my opinion, but for Aunt Sylvia time would have dragged if it had not been for Mrs Ambrose. She it was who had the excellent notion that later on in the year, we might travel.

"It does sound rather nice, Mrs Ambrose, but I am afraid it would prove too difficult an undertaking, would it not, Autumn?" Aunt Sylvia said.

"Why should it? Oh, arrangements would have to be made, true, but I think it is an excellent idea!" I replied.

"Sir James would never accompany us!" my aunt demurred.

"We do not know whether he would or not, until we ask him," I said sensibly. "It will be some time later in the year if we do go, and by then I should imagine his mysterious invention will be completed. Who knows, it might suit him very well to travel abroad with us!"

"Oh, I do hope so! Do you know, I feel cheered already by the very thought of it!" Aunt Sylvia exclaimed. "Time passes quite pleasantly here, but one day is so much like another. This would be something to which we could look forward! Of course, we would not wish to be gay, it would not be seemly: but sight-seeing is quite permissible, even whilst one is in mourning! Just think, we could see some of the wonderful places of which we have read, and before we went we should have all the planning to do: how we should travel, and where we should go, and that is almost as nice as actually going!"

"You have not been abroad before, Lady Kimberley?" asked Mrs Ambrose.

"Yes, once. When I was a very young girl, only just out, my Mama took me to Paris," my aunt replied.

"Ah, The City of Romance, I know it well! I am so pleased that you and Miss Kimberley are prepared to consider the idea. If you decide to go, and when you have chosen which countries you would like to visit, then a route could be determined. Italy and France I know best of the European countries, although I possess some slight knowledge of several others. To travel later in the year is ideal, as summer is not the best of seasons for delicate English complexions to take themselves to countries bordering on the Mediterranean!"

The thought of a trip abroad gave us a new interest; something to discuss and plan after dinner during the lovely summer evenings which followed. Somewhat to my surprise Uncle James agreed to accompany us without hesitation, and expressed his approval of Mrs Ambrose's excellent idea.

"Unless I am much mistaken, my work will be completed in a very few weeks from now," he said. "But if some catastrophe does occur and I find my calculations are at fault, then I must start again, and when I do so will be immaterial!"

The prospect of visiting and seeing with my own eyes places of which before I had only read, I found most attractive, and yet I did not wish to leave Drawbridge Court for too great a length of time. I was torn between the desires of wishing to go, yet wanting to stay! What if anything should go wrong whilst I was away: would those who remained be able to manage without me? Of course, it was pure vanity on my part: Mr Biggs was quite capable of seeing to the estate business, and Mrs Wilkes and Dixon were more than able to attend to the smooth running of the house; added to which Mr Dawson the solicitor would keep an eye on things, and would probably journey down here occasionally to make sure that all was well. Legally, I had no business being in charge of the estate. If it had not been for the fact that Uncle James was content to let me take command, more than a year must pass before I could give any effective orders at all!

* * *

"Dear me, Lady Kimberley, there does not appear to be another skein of that pretty rose silk thread in your workbasket!" Mrs Ambrose remarked one evening. "Will you have enough to finish the embroidery on which you are working? I notice that rose is the predominant colour!"

"Are you sure, Mrs Ambrose?" Aunt Sylvia sounded dismayed. "I had thought there were two or three more skeins of that shade of silk."

"There does not appear to be. Just let me lift the work-tray up so that I can make sure that nothing has fallen through to the wrong compartment: no, I am afraid there is no more left!"

"But I have all of this flower, and the posy in the corner to do yet!" my aunt exclaimed. "Oh, how utterly vexing!"

"My dear Sylvia, pray do not sound so aggrieved," Uncle James smiled. "You can purchase more, surely?"

"Yes, but it means going all the way into Rochester, or sending someone to match it for me," my aunt exclaimed.

"Then let us go into Rochester," I suggested. "Let us go early one morning and make a day of it. We could have luncheon at The Crown, purchase your embroidery silk, and do a little personal shopping as well. There are several things which I require, and I expect Mrs Ambrose and you, too, can think of some things which your wardrobes lack!"

"That would make a pleasant change!" Aunt Sylvia brightened. "Do you not think so, Mrs Ambrose?"

"Indeed I do! When do you suggest that we go?"

"We could go tomorrow if it is fine," I said. "If the weather should be inclement, we can go on the first suitable day after that."

"It is market day tomorrow!" Aunt Sylvia reminded me.

"Well, that does not signify," I replied. "When I suggested that we set out early, I did not mean at the crack of dawn, and by the time we reach Rochester, most of the market folk will have transacted their business and be returning to their homes. We should naturally bespeak a private parlour in which to take our luncheon, and in the afternoon the shops we shall visit will be no more crowded than they are normally! Of course, if you should prefer it we can go on another day!"

"Oh no, Autumn, what you say is true enough. Now if you will excuse me, I think I shall retire. Mrs Ambrose, if you are not too tired I would be grateful if you will come up with me to help make out a list of the things which I require. Your handwriting is so much clearer than mine, and if you will help me the task will be completed in no time at all!"

"Certainly, Lady Kimberley, I shall be delighted to assist you. Then I too must see what I need to purchase. I do think these outings planned on the spur of the moment are so much more enjoyable than those which are arranged weeks ahead! Good night, Miss Kimberley, Sir James."

"Good night, Autumn, I suggest you retire early as well if we are to set out betimes tomorrow," advised my aunt.

"Yes, I think I shall. Good night, Aunt Sylvia, Mrs Ambrose, Uncle James. Come, Carlin, I shall play with you for a little longer than usual tonight to make up for the fact that you will be left behind tomorrow!"

The dawn chorus awoke me, and I lay and listened to the song of the birds as the sky brightened to give promise of another lovely day ahead. Thinking to give Carlin a treat I rose, made my toilette, and said:

"Come along, Carlin, we shall go for a walk whilst the day is young."

But the little dog feigned slumber! I could see his eyes gleaming at me from behind barely opened lids, then he gave a snort, a gentle snore, and settled himself even more comfortably in his basket.

"Up, lazybones!" I laughed. "Come along. You can sleep for all of the day after I have departed for Rochester!" and reluctantly he obeyed me and waddled behind me to the door with a look of utmost resignation upon his wrinkled little face.

It was still too early for breakfast when we returned to the house so we entered by way of the kitchens where I knew tea was always a-brewing at this time in the morning, and although our entrance caused a momentary flurry, soon I was sitting in Cook's chair at the huge scrubbed table as I had done many times when I was a little girl and had gone forth in the dawn to return with a ravenous appetite.

"Let me send you a tea-tray into the breakfast parlour, Miss Autumn," Cook offered. "It will take no more than a minute to prepare."

"No, thank you," I replied. "It is so long since I was in your kitchen at this early hour! Let us pretend I am a little girl again, and that you are regaling me with that strong, sweet tea as you used to: and I would not refuse some bread and honey! Do you remember how you always gave me bread and honey?"

"Indeed I do, Miss," she smiled. "It seems only yesterday!"

And so I feasted as in days of yore, and Carlin had

his first taste of honey, for which he immediately developed a lasting passion.

We had planned to make an early start, but by the time my aunt's shopping list, which had somehow been misplaced, was located, and I had remembered at the last moment that I had no money with me, the morning was well advanced. Then Mrs Ambrose said:

"One minute, ladies, if you please. Has anyone thought to bring a sample of the rose silk thread which we are making this journey to match?"

"I have not, have you, Autumn?"

"Why should I? My dear aunt, it is your embroidery, is it not?"

We stared at each other, and then began to laugh helplessly.

"Well, honestly!" I said at last. "Who would believe it to be possible that we should forget the reason for our going? I will fetch it, and then perhaps we can set off!"

As I had predicted, when we neared Rochester a steady stream of traffic was leaving the city: we decided to leave the carriage at The Crown, bespeak our luncheon and a private parlour, execute a little shopping, and then return to the inn for the meal.

"Actually, I do not have a great many items to purchase," announced my aunt. "Let me see, I must visit the haberdashers, the milliners, the glovers, the drapers, and then I thought it would be nice to see what books on travel are available. Those we have at Drawbridge Court are sadly behind the times!"

"Well, shall we go to the drapers and the haberdashers, buy what we want from them, return to the inn for luncheon, and then spend the rest of the afternoon at the other shops?" I suggested. "If we leave the bookshop until last, we can browse in peace knowing that the rest of our shopping is completed."

"That would be capital! We had better stay close together, as the streets are rather crowded. Come then, let us be about our business."

Although it was an ordinary market day, there seemed to be a holiday spirit abroad in the air: the serious business was over for most folk, the haggling and dickering had been completed and now was the time for enjoyment. The weather was fine: everyone seemed to be in good humour as women with heavy baskets, men with sacks or bales upon their shoulders, and children with boxes on wheels all pushed and jostled their way to their destinations. There was every kind of vehicle upon the road: huge wagons drawn by mighty Shire horses, farm carts, gigs, carriages and hand-carts: there was even a hearse which I was a little relieved to see had no occupant: all embarking upon their homeward journeys at what pace they could muster, to the accompaniment of mostly jovial badinage although there was the odd choicely appropriate insult or colourful curse offered, and even the occasional missile!

"I think we had better return to the inn for our luncheon, and do our shopping afterwards," my aunt had to raise her voice to be heard above the din. "Let us retrace our steps. I for one am heartily tired of my bonnet being knocked askew!"

"Yes, the streets will be quieter this afternoon." I turned to Mrs Ambrose, who had been walking slightly behind us. "My aunt suggest that we return to The Crown and do our shopping later," I said.

Without any real surprise I discovered we had become separated amidst the crowds, but I knew she could not be far away as we had only traversed a short distance from the inn, and I did not think it possible that Mrs Ambrose could have overtaken us.

"Oh dear, have we lost Mrs Ambrose?" asked Aunt Sylvia.

"Only for the moment," I replied. "We shall soon find her. We cannot miss her if we turn back now!"

From that minute all was confusion and the bright sunny day was changed instantly to one of a nightmare quality, terminating in total darkness! The pavement on which Aunt Sylvia and I were standing was narrow: the traffic was exceptionally heavy, and some of it was travelling at too fast a pace to be conducive with safety: and somehow, I was in the middle of it! I had a vague impression of someone pushing or of something falling against me, so that I was hurled directly into the path of a pair of horses which were drawing an oncoming carriage. The fact that I was not killed outright was a miracle; and as I fell the sight which met my terrified gaze I shall remember for all of my days, and even now it comes to haunt my dreams. Great dapple-grey horses were rearing above me: their iron-shod hooves descending relentlessly to crush the life from my body; and they had nowhere to land but upon my person as I lay directly beneath them! Somebody was screaming! The horses were whinnying their panic; but before I had even time to breathe the name of God, He in His infinite mercy, granted that I should know no more!

The room in which I opened my eyes was dim and unfamiliar, then I realized that the curtains were drawn against the rays of the westering sun which managed to intrude its presence through a chink here and there. Someone was sitting near my bed, but as I attempted to move my head so that I might discover who this was, a stab of pure agony took away my breath with its intensity so that involuntarily I groaned.

"Autumn? Autumn, my love, I am here," Aunt Sylvia's dear voice reached me through a mist of pain, and I was comforted.

"Where am I? What has happened?" I whispered.

"You have had an accident, dear, but although you have been hurt, the extent of your injuries are not serious. We are at the Vicarage of St Martin's Church here in Rochester. We came here yesterday, and we are to remain here as guests until you are well enough to travel!"

"How badly hurt am I?"

"There is a nasty bump upon your head, your collar-bone is broken, and the doctor thinks at least two of your ribs are cracked. You have wrenched your ankle as well. Do you remember what happened?"

"Yes. I thought that death was upon me! It is unbelievable that I should be trampled by horses, and yet live!" I replied.

"Well, you were not exactly trampled, my pet. The young curate attached to this church dragged you clear of the horses' hooves, well almost clear. That was the act of a hero, indeed! Now you must drink this, and then you should sleep until morning. Do not fear, you will not be left alone. Either the vicar's wife, Mrs Ambrose, or I shall be with you all through the night, although the doctor assures me that after you drink this, you will not stir till tomorrow!"

So obediently, I drank the surprisingly pleasant-tasting concoction and drifted off to a dreamless slumber.

The Rev. and Mrs Howells made us so very welcome during the weeks that followed, that every time I think of them a glow comes to my heart. They were the stuff of which true Christians are made, and although comparatively poor, they gave with open hands to all in need. The invasion of the Kimberleys ruffled them not a jot, and although some of the luxury to which I was accustomed at Drawbridge Court was lacking here, the joyous spirit that permeated the whole Vicarage more than atoned for any slight discomforts suffered.

Our host and hostess were a childless, middle-aged couple who regarded Robin Weston, the young curate, as their own son: and indeed, a young man of such courage and presence of mind was a son of whom to be proud! Martha was the domestic tower of strength, and with just the youthful and untrained Jenny to aid her, she managed to keep the wheels of the household running smoothly. Mrs Howells did not consider herself above performing any domestic task, and I suppose that until the Kimberleys descended on the Vicarage they existed quite comfortably, even if trivial chores were ignored from time to time.

"The Lord's work is of more importance than dust upon the mantel-shelf!" Mrs Howells smiled when once Aunt Sylvia asked her how she managed to run the house and bring comfort to the poor in the parish at the same time. "There will be dust and grime in the world long after I am gone. It is people who are important, Lady Kimberley! Their woes and worries and sufferings merit my attention far more than does the odd untidy room!"

But let me hasten to add that the Vicarage was clean in every respect, although often cushions needed plumping, or books and newspapers were left where a reader had set them down when called away upon important business elsewhere.

Well, the influx of the Kimberleys soon altered the pleasantly disorganized life at the Vicarage. Whilst I was still too ill to care, all arrangements were made by Aunt Sylvia. If Mrs Howells did perhaps wonder whether she was straining the resources of the Vicarage a little too far, she agreed to any proposition made by my aunt; but she need not have feared. My aunt is a sensible lady who knew that a staff of just one woman and a young girl could not possibly attend to all our needs, so she sent for Miriam and Bertha. They would bring our clothes and toilette necessities, and they cheerfully undertook to work under Martha's direction in the kitchen and about the house.

"I know that ladies' maids are not supposed to soil their hands with menial tasks, Miss," Bertha informed me once she had arrived. "But there! In a case like this Miriam and me don't mind!"

I smiled to myself. It was not so long since Bertha had been nervous of handling my gowns, and now here she was giving herself airs!

"That is extremely kind of you both," I replied.

"Well, Miss, it wouldn't do for nobody to maid you but me! If I speak truth I will say that I quite like being here. Oh, I do not mean that I am glad you are hurt, Miss, but when Miriam and me are free of an evening we can take a walk about the city. It makes a change for us!"

There remained the question of how we could reimburse the vicar and his wife for the expenses they were incurring on our behalf. We could not possibly offer them money, but five extra mouths to feed would make an enormous difference to their household budget, we knew.

"Perhaps if we asked our housekeeper to send some provisions, saying they are fresh from the home-farm, or grown and reared on our own land they might be acceptable?" I suggested to Aunt Sylvia.

"That is an excellent idea, Autumn. Acceptable or not, something must be done! We are eating the poor woman out of house and home!"

My bones were mending nicely: the lump upon my head had subsided and my ankle had healed completely. I was allowed to leave my bed for a short period each day, and when I was fit to be seen by a gentleman I asked that Mr Weston the curate might come to my chamber, so that I could thank him for saving my life.

I had envisaged him as tall, powerfully built, and were not all heroes handsome? But when he stood before me, I had to marshal my wits if I was not to betray my surprise at his appearance. He was a little man: if I had been standing, his head might have reached the height of my ear, but I doubt it: in the assumption that he was powerfully built I had been correct, the breadth of his shoulders was remarkable! He had light brown hair, a nondescript countenance, and woefully large ears that made themselves extremely obvious by protruding from his head at right-angles; but when he smiled his eyes twinkled at you, and his mouth relaxed in the most engaging grin, so that you forgot his looks completely as you felt yourself enveloped by warmth and goodness.

"Mr Weston, do pray be seated," I said. "I am so pleased to see you, particularly so that I may thank you for saving my life at the grave risk of your own."

"You are kind to say so, Miss Kimberley, but I must be truthful. The man who is really responsible for us both being here today is the coachman who was driving the carriage. How he held those horses I do not know, but hold them he did, thereby nearly giving me time to pull you clear of their hooves. Nearly, but also not quite! You were struck a glancing blow just before I had you safe, but it could have been much worse!"

"Much worse? It would certainly have been fatal for me if you had not been there!" I exclaimed. "Come, Mr Weston, the coachman might have held his beasts in a truly wonderful way, but if it had not been for your brave action, I should surely have met my Maker that day!"

"Only if He willed it, ma'am. As you see, it was not so. I was sent to do what I could at that particular moment. It was the Hand of God, Miss Kimberley!"

"Yes, I know, but it was also your hands which saved me from a dreadful end, Mr Weston, so do not be so modest," I smiled.

"Well, I am proud that you should thank me for my action, when I know I was sent to perform it," the young man laughed. "It is not every day I am able to assist a beautiful maiden in distress: I shall remember that one for a very long time! Heroes with looks such as mine and lovely damsels in dire need do not often go hand in hand, but on that occasion they did! Let us say, all is well that ends well!"

Uncle James drove over from Drawbridge Court to see for himself how I was faring, bringing with him an ecstatic Carlin.

"Autumn, take this animal of yours in charge once more, I beg of you," he said. "He has given us no peace at Drawbridge Court! He has moped and whined, been off his food, and has taken to following me about like an uneasy conscience! He cries to be let out, and he is no sooner out than he cries to be let in again. Nobody would think that he is only a dog! He has upset the whole house with his whims and fads: even Dixon has been crawling about the floor, trying to coax him to eat minced chicken!"

But now he was content! He lay quivering in my lap: occasionally staring up into my face to reassure himself that it was really I, and that he had found his mistress at last!

The time came for us to make our departure from the Vicarage and its kindly occupants. We could not insult these people by offering to pay for their hospitality, but Uncle James and Aunt Sylvia had gleaned the information from the vicar and his wife that the parish was a very poor one, and there were so many worthy people living in it whom they would dearly like to help more than their financial resources would permit. Here was a way to show our gratitude which would be quite acceptable, and when Uncle James made his donation to the church poor-box, the vicar was almost overcome.

"Sir James, this is a truly noble gift!" he stammered. "Oh, what wonderful work my wife and I will be able to do with a princely sum like this! Thank you, sir, thank you!"

"And thank you, Mr Howells, and your lady wife! Let us not say farewell. From time to time, you shall hear from the Kimberleys!"

And so it is that as regularly as the season of Christmas approaches, so a wagon can be seen trundling its way from Drawbridge Court to the Vicarage of St Martin's, Rochester, heavy laden with things to make merry the heart of man so that our friends may indulge freely in their favourite pastime: the joy of giving!

SEVEN

EVERY time I return to Drawbridge Court after an absence of more than a few days, I am struck afresh by its comfort and beauty. Oh, it is not to everyone's taste, I know: some folk prefer a more modern building in which to live, and cannot understand why I should so love such an old house; but for me the age of my home adds to its charm. Also I know that my family have lived at Drawbridge Court in an unbroken line since it was first completed: loving hands have added things here, and altered things there, sometimes with incongruous results; but I would not have the house any other way than that which it is.

My assumption had been proved correct that things could be run very well in my absence, and the only tasks which needed extra attention were those of bringing the household accounts and estate books up to date, and of correcting various errors made in them by Uncle James, who had misguidedly tried to see to this business during the time I had lain injured in Rochester.

"I am sorry, Autumn, but I am afraid that I have got them a little muddled," Uncle James apologized.

"That does not matter," I smiled. "It will not take me long to set them to rights."

The subject of foreign travel seemed to have been forgotten for the moment, and I was content to let it remain that way. To be in my home, and to spend my days peacefully amidst familiar surroundings was all that I desired, for I found that although my body was healed, my nerves were not so steady as I had always known them to be. On the first few occasions when I went to the stables after my return home, I had to steel myself before I could even approach a horse! The creatures seemed to sense my lack of confidence, and became uneasy and restless in their stalls when I was nearby; and when I went riding for the first time after my accident, I had to really brace myself before I could mount my dear little mare and I knew she had no vices whatsoever!

It took no more than a few days to conquer these fears, and soon I was as frequently in the saddle as I had been before. Often in the early mornings I would rise, and once I was clad in my riding-habit Carlin would snuggle deeper into his basket: when he saw me attired thus he knew he could not accompany me, and would be content to remain where he was until my return. As I only rode on my own estate I did not deem it necessary for a groom to follow wherever I went, and once I had left the house behind me I rejoiced in the solitude of the fresh summer dawns when it seemed that I alone was astir.

But was I alone during these early morning rides? Gradually there came upon me the feeling that I was being followed! I would rein in my mare suddenly and hear the thud of hooves behind me, but always they halted before the rider came into sight. Once I turned and rode back the way I had come so that I might catch a glimpse of my pursuer, but this stratagem was only rewarded by hearing the sound of some creature making haste to conceal itself in the cover of a small wood which happened to be nearby. It could have been a mounted horse, or on the other hand it could have been a wild animal.

"Who is there? Come forth and show yourself!" I had called in what I had hoped was a confident voice, but there was only the sighing of a slight breeze to answer my summons.

Oh, it was too ridiculous to merit serious consideration! My nerves were getting the better of me, and I would have to control these imaginings if I was not to become frightened of every shadow! The most trivial things began to irritate me. Lady Mary Brett had asked if we could find a place amongst our staff for a faithful retainer of a friend of theirs.

"These friends of ours have suffered financial reverses and have had to retrench," she had explained. "They have asked me if I could place a few of their servants for them. Only those who have been with them for a great length of time! Sir Hedworth and I are taking one or two, and if you see your way to employing this footman, it would be such a help!"

"Well, if he is a good man I am sure Dixon could find a use for him," my aunt had replied. "I think it most commendable, that these friends of whom you speak should spare a thought for their servants, when they obviously have other worries!"

And so Luker entered our service: he was well-trained, deferential, and Dixon thought highly of him; but there was that about the man I could not like! One is not supposed to like or dislike servants I know, they are merely there to do one's bidding; but here at Drawbridge Court we regard them in a different light. This man Luker was all that a footman should be, and as a stranger to the house I suppose he was anxious to learn his way around, but I found his method of doing so most provoking. Wherever I went, he seemed to be there as well! I would glance up from the hall to find him regarding me from the head of the stairs: whenever I emerged from my chamber he would be in the upstairs corridor, not near my door, but certainly within sight of it: he would be hovering nearby when I came from the study after my duties were done in the morning, and once I walked the length of the house to go to the music room for some trivial reason, and when I came forth from there Luker was again close at hand! Perhaps he was trying to impress me with his attentiveness: he might have felt unsure of his new position in which he had been placed, and was doing his best to please; but far from doing so, he began to annoy me beyond measure!

"Aunt Sylvia, what do you think of this new man, Luker?" I asked her a week or so after he had taken up his position with us.

"I think he is an excellent servant, my dear. Why do you ask?"

"Oh, for no particular reason. It is only that he always seems to be underfoot! Have you not noticed?"

"I cannot say I have. He performs his duties admirably, from what I can see. Has Dixon complained of him?"

"On the contrary. Dixon commends him, and his work. It is just that Luker always seems to be at hand!"

"But that is what he is engaged for, dear!" My aunt regarded me in a puzzled manner.

"Oh, I am being silly," I said. "Luker is a good footman and came to us with first-class references."

"Yes, and why you notice his presence so much is because he is new to our service," Aunt Sylvia explained sensibly. "The other staff have been here for so long that you do not even notice them!"

Of course, that was the reason! I should have thought of it myself, instead of letting my frayed nerves get the better of my common-sense! But that did not account for the uncomfortable sensation that I was being followed when I went riding early in the day!

It was my determination to conquer these stupid fancies of mine that introduced me to a stranger, and caused me to be absent from Drawbridge Court when once more tragedy struck our once happy home: bringing with it grief, shock, and the dreadful suspicion that the presence of evil was amongst us.

The sun was glittering brightly upon the early morning dew as I left the house one fine day, and made my way towards open country where I could give the mare her head. We had spent a restless night, Carlin and I; but now he was fast asleep in his basket, whereas I was fully awake. Twice he had disturbed me: once by growling and running to sniff under my chamber door when the night was yet young; then he had settled down and I had fallen asleep to be startled into wakefulness by his bark, and then his pleas to be lifted up beside me.

"What is wrong, Carlin?" I had asked the little dog, and he had whimpered and run to the door, so donning a robe I opened it to see if aught was amiss. But no, the house was silent: I listened intently and then sniffed to see if there was any smell of smoke. Heroic dogs of which I had read saved sleeping households from being burned to death in their beds, or from some other disaster. Not so Carlin! Far from showing any inclination towards bravery he was doing his very best to leap on to my vacated bed, but his little bandy legs would not give him enough impetus to succeed in this undertaking.

"There is nothing there!" I scolded. "You are a naughty dog to awaken me for no reason! No, you shall not get up there! Into your basket, sir, this instant!"

So with tail a-droop and a look of utter resignation upon his crinkled face, he waddled across the room to curl up in his basket, emitting a deep sigh as he did so. The dog was becoming as neurotic as I was, or downright naughty; but I smiled as I recalled these crafty antics of his, although at the time I had been cross with the little animal.

My thoughts were busy as I rode and at first I was sure I was alone, but after a time I felt that the unwelcome presence was once more behind me. I did not draw rein altogether but checked the pace of my mount, and at last I saw him! It was only a fleeting glimpse, but enough to show me that my imagination had not been playing tricks after all! The thick-set, brown-clad figure was mounted on a bay, but no sooner had I seen the mysterious rider than he disappeared from view behind a clump of trees.

Normally I would have returned the way I had come and confronted him; but the certain knowledge that I had indeed been pursued, and that if he had nothing to hide he would have ridden up and given me the time of day, set me trembling. If I approached that clump of trees he might spring on me! He and I were alone, with no friendly soul to succour me if I should call for aid. Through my mind raced the memory of the unexplained footprints on the roof at the time the chimney had fallen. Dixon and I had suspected that a madman might be at work, and then dismissed the idea as being absurd: but what if we had been right? Then how I came to be thrust so suddenly under those horses' hooves in Rochester was another puzzle; and poor Grandpapa's death had never been accounted for, either!

Fearless? Intrepid? No, these are not the words to describe the next actions of Miss Autumn Kimberley: this was too fine a day to test my bravery and finish my life lying dead in a ditch, I decided, so I touched my mare sharply with my heel and made what speed I could muster away from that clump of trees and the sinister presence which they concealed. But my troubles had only just begun, for my panic must have communicated itself to my mare: she took the bit between her teeth and bolted, and although I am an experienced horsewoman, soon I found that she was completely out of control and I was clinging to the reins for dear life!

It seemed an age before my mount tired sufficiently for me to even consider regaining mastery of her; but when the time came, I had other fears to distract me. From behind came the sound of pounding hooves! Nearer, ever nearer they came: whoever was following me had taken advantage of the situation, and now that my mare was tired I was almost within his power! Yes: at last my mount was tiring, but instead of reining her in I drove her on! But it was useless: relentlessly, my pursuer closed the gap between us, and I gripped my riding crop tightly so that I might defend myself when he had me within his grasp. If my life was to be forfeit, I should sell it dearly, I vowed!

He was directly behind me: it could only be a matter of moments before he could reach my mare's bridle, and then I almost fainted with sheer relief! The beast which was drawing level with mine was a roan, not a bay; and instead of a menacing arm clad in brown coming into my line of vision, the arm that effortlessly took control of my mare was clad in dark blue!

I gazed up into the face of a complete stranger: obviously a gentleman from his gleaming riding-boots to the crown of his modish top-hat which he raised to me, as he asked in a voice quick with concern:

"Are you all right, Miss Kimberley?"

"Yes, sir, I am indeed, thanks to you!" Actually, it was quite the reverse: I should have been far better off without his intervention, but how could I tell him so?

"There is a fallen log yonder. If you will allow me to help you dismount, perhaps you might rest upon it until you are somewhat recovered from what must have been an unnerving experience," he suggested.

"That is kind of you, sir," I replied. "Yes, I shall be pleased to do so."

He lifted me from the saddle and gave me the support of his arm until I reached the log, then he said:

"I will walk the horses so that they do not become chilled after that wild chase."

He left me to compose myself and as my shaking limbs gradually ceased their trembling, I watched him as he led the horses back and forth a short distance from where I was sitting. I was intrigued: here was a gentleman who knew me, he had called me by name; and yet I could not remember meeting him! He was young, perhaps in his early twenties: tall, slender, and his dark blue frock-coat and white riding breeches were of the finest cut. When he had doffed his hat to me he had revealed dark curling hair, and his eyes were a startling blue, fringed by lashes of which any woman might have been proud. Ah, I must have met him whilst I was in London! Smugly, I thought that I must have made a greater impression on him than he had on me; for he had known me instantly, whereas I recalled him not at all! No: that was not quite the truth: his face was familiar, but I could not put a name to it and I was still trying to remember where it was we had met when he led up the horses and enquired:

"How are you now, ma'am? Do you feel able to mount your mare, or do you prefer to rest for a little longer?"

"I am quite recovered, sir, thank you," I replied. "If

you will add to your kindness by assisting me into the saddle, I shall be even more in your debt!"

"Debt, ma'am? I count it a privilege to be of service!" He cupped his palm to receive my heel, then he too mounted and we started on the return journey to Drawbridge Court.

"I beg your forgiveness, sir. I am sure I know you, yet I am afraid that I cannot call your name to mind," I said as we trotted homewards.

"There is nothing to forgive, Miss Kimberley," he replied, and smiled at the puzzled look which must have been evident on my face. "No, ma'am, we have not met ere this morning!"

"Well, you know me, sir! You have called me by name! And I am sure that I have seen you somewhere before!"

"Perhaps you have, Miss Kimberley, who can say? Of one thing I am certain. If we had ever been formally introduced, the occasion would still be fresh in my memory!"

"Then how does it come about that you know me by name?" I demanded.

"Who does not know of the beautiful Miss Kimberley? She of the flaming hair who resides at Drawbridge Court?" he laughed.

"Flaming, sir?" I frowned my displeasure. "The shade of my hair is commonly known as auburn!"

"Just so! Commonly! But there is nothing common about Miss Kimberley, or her hair. Hair the colour of leaping flames! Do you not think that is far more romantic a description than mere auburn, or dare I say it, ginger?"

This conversation with a complete stranger was becoming a trifle too personal, so to change the subject I asked:

"You are staying in the neighbourhood, sir? You have friends hereabouts?"

"No, ma'am, I am just exploring the countryside in a leisurely way."

"Exploring? Then you are a stranger to Kent?" He had a slight accent which was not that of a foreigner, but I could not even begin to guess from where he came.

"As you say, Miss Kimberley, I am a stranger to Kent."

I was relieved to see we were nearing Drawbridge Court. To talk to this gentleman was proving to be most difficult. My companion volunteered no information regarding himself or his background, and the conversation seemed to be developing into an interrogation on my part, and a series of evasive answers upon his!

"My home will be within sight in a few minutes," I remarked. "It will please me greatly if you will enter it, and perhaps take breakfast with us."

"I shall be pleased to see Drawbridge Court," he answered. "But I am afraid I must refuse your invitation to enter it. This morning I am somewhat pressed for time. Perhaps on another occasion?"

"Oh, dear, I am so sorry to have detained you, if time is a matter of moment!" I was genuinely contrite. "You gave me no hint of the fact that I was hindering you."

"And neither were you, Miss Kimberley. Even if you had it would have been time well spent, but you have not. It is just that I have an appointment, which I can keep punctually if I leave you now. On another day I shall be pleased to call, if I may?"

"Do, sir, and you will be most welcome," I replied, and then the house was before us.

"So this is Drawbridge Court!" my companion remarked, and we sat in silence regarding my dear home.

"You sound as though the place has been described to you!" I observed, eventually.

"Yes, it has been. Many times. It is just as I imagined it would be! And now I must say farewell, Miss Kimberley."

"Farewell, sir, and once again, thank you for riding to my rescue."

He smiled, raised his hat, then trotted away in the direction of the village whilst I slowly rode towards the house.

The stables lay behind Drawbridge Court, and as we had approached from the front I must ride halfway around the house before I reached them. My thoughts were occupied with the gentleman who had just left me, and I realized that even now, I did not know his name! Why should he have been so evasive. He had been as polite and respectful as he should have been certainly, but still I did not know who he was! He had answered my questions in a teasing manner, but although I was curious as to his identity I could not press him for a serious reply; it would have been most unmannerly! If he wished to intrigue me he had succeeded; and I was pondering upon his unusual behaviour when from the house came a sound like a clap of thunder!

My mare, tired as she was, reared and nearly unseated me; and if I had not held her firmly, I am sure that she would have found the strength from somewhere to bolt once again! The sound had come from the west wing, and I rounded the corner of the house to see that nearly every pane of glass had been shattered, and that smoke was issuing from where there had been windows! There were screams and cries of terror: somebody was shouting for help and I slid from the saddle and gave my mare a sharp slap upon the rump in the hope that she would find her own way to the stables, whilst I tried to enter the house.

As I opened a small side door I was immediately driven back by the smoke and fumes which belched forth, so I closed it hurriedly and sprinted round to the front of the house. There all was confusion, and I grabbed the arm of a scurrying footman and demanded:

"What is amiss?"

"God knows, Miss! Something is to do in the west wing, but what I cannot say!"

"Then we shall find out!" I shouted above the din. "Follow me!"

As we went I spied Dixon through the clouds of smoke, which although dense enough were not so dense as the smoke which had poured from the west wing when I tried to enter there.

"There's a fire, Miss! In the west wing," he informed me, unnecessarily.

"All of the women out of the house, Dixon," I said. "And all of the men to the east wing for buckets of water. Quickly now! Where is my aunt?"

"I do not know, Miss."

"Well, go about your business and I shall do my best to find her," I instructed. "You, stay with me please," this last to the footman whom I had encountered when I had entered the house.

We made our way along the main downstairs corridor, past fleeing maidservants and men hurrying to the east wing for water. Every bucketful must be transported across the courtyard and as I went I prayed that nobody had been hurt, and that the damage would not be too great.

Suddenly I saw my aunt and Mrs Ambrose: they too were striving to enter the west wing and were being driven back by the smoke and fumes, which although thick enough to defeat their progress were not so dense as they had been. Coughing, choking, gallantly the two ladies were trying to reach the seat of the fire: they had not yet seen me, and I caught each one by the gown.

"Let be! Come away!" I attempted to say, but could only cough and gesticulate.

"James!" Aunt Sylvia managed to gasp. "He must be in there somewhere!"

Gradually the atmosphere cleared sufficiently to allow us to effect an entrance; and when we discovered that the house was only superficially damaged on the ground floor, my heart was sick with dread. In the cellars lay Uncle James's laboratory and before we even opened the massive door which led to it, I knew what we should find!

Yes, the noise which had almost deafened me ere I entered the house was caused by an explosion! Noxious fumes and smoke once more filled the passageway as we opened the laboratory door, and we could hear the crackle of flames! There were heroes amongst our staff. One man, whom I fleetingly recognized as Luker, said:

"Make way! I am going down there!" And with a soaking blanket enveloping him he led the way, and several others followed his example.

Fearfully we clung together, my aunt and I, and slowly the seconds passed until we could hear the sound of heavy footsteps stumbling up the stone staircase. I held Aunt Sylvia's trembling body close as the first man appeared in the doorway; but with head bent low he shuffled past us, and would not meet our eyes.

"James!" Aunt Sylvia shrieked, and tried to tear herself from my grasp; but I gripped her tightly, so that she could not plunge into the swirling smoke and fumes which were issuing from the stairway.

Another man emerged: this time it was Luker the footman who had unwittingly incurred my displeasure, but today he had given me cause to be grateful to him for his presence of mind and courage. He had the fortitude to face us squarely, but sadly he shook his head.

"Sir James?" faltered my aunt.

"There's naught to be done for the master, my lady," he said gently. "He is beyond our aid!"

I felt her plump little body go limp within my arms.

"Quickly!" I cried. "Her ladyship has fainted! Somebody help me with her!"

Willing hands took her from me and I said:

"Carry her ladyship to her chamber. Mrs Ambrose, attend my aunt if you please."

It was a blessing that she should swoon! When my aunt had been borne away, I asked of the men who had descended the steps:

"Is the fire still raging down there?"

"It's burning, Miss, but not what you might call raging!" replied one of them. "There's more smoke than fire, like!"

"But my uncle? Has he not been burned?"

"Yes, Miss, but not so badly as we feared."

"He may be alive, then!" I cried. "For the love of God do not just stand there. Bring him up!"

"Nay, Miss, there is no life in his poor body. I knows the face of death when I sees it! Come lads, let us bring up the master, and then we'll put out that bit o' fire!"

The flickering hope that he might yet live was proved to be forlorn when they carried Uncle James's lifeless form up the stone steps: the stone steps which only he had trod in many a long year. His hair and eyebrows had been singed away: his face and hands were severely burned; but the conflagration had not been fierce enough to cause his death by flame, it was the smoke which had taken his life! The swirling, choking, blinding, foul-smelling smoke and fumes had suffocated my poor dear uncle, and in the laboratory where he had spent so many contented hours, he had met his death!

"Take him to my grandfather's old chamber," I instructed those who bore him, and with tears making clean little channels upon their begrimed faces, tenderly they carried him up the main staircase and laid him on the great bed which had known no occupant since my grandsire had rested there not so very long ago.

The fire was soon dealt with: the walls, floor and ceiling in the laboratory were of stone: the only inflammable objects were the scant furnishings. Just a large desk, shelves and bookcases, several tables and chairs, and some wooden scaffolding which had obviously supported complicated apparatus of some kind, but broken glass was everywhere.

Mrs Wilkes was at my elbow.

"Miss, there is a tray of tea awaiting you in the study," she said. "I have sent it there as it is the chamber furthest away from the west wing. Go and refresh yourself, Miss. We others can see to what needs to be done here, and Dixon has sent for the doctor."

"Thank you, Mrs Wilkes," I replied, and as one in a daze I made my way to the sanctuary of the study: there to pour and sip my tea, my mind occupied with all kinds of trivial things as though to blot out the dreadful disaster with which we had just been smitten. After a while there was a light tap upon the study door and Mrs Ambrose entered.

"How is my aunt?" I asked quickly.

"She is asleep, Miss Kimberley. I gave her some of her drops. The poor soul was so distraught that I thought it was for the best!"

"That was very wise, Mrs Ambrose," I said. "Thank you."

"I do not think Lady Kimberley will awaken before this evening," Mrs Ambrose told me, then asked, "Shall I remain here with you, Miss Kimberley?"

"I prefer to be alone if you do not mind," I replied. "You too need some rest, Mrs Ambrose!"

She nodded. "As you wish. I shall see you later in the day, but I shall be in my chamber if you desire my presence before then."

But my wish for solitude was not granted, for no sooner had Mrs Ambrose departed than there was another knock upon the door. This time it was Bertha, clutching a wriggling dog in her arms. Her face was blotched with weeping and she gulped before she spoke.

"I'm sorry, Miss, but he would see you! Shall I take him away, or leave him?"

"He may remain, Bertha," I replied. "Carlin will be out of the way in here."

"Thank you, Miss."

I was still sitting numbly in my chair when Sir Hedworth Brett was announced.

"My dear Autumn, what terrible news is this I hear? Can what I have been told be true?" he asked in a shocked voice.

I rose and stood staring mutely into his well-loved countenance. I could not speak, but the expression on my face must have told him that what he had heard was true enough. Sir Hedworth reached forth his hands to me, and without conscious thought I ran to him, and found I was being clasped in his comforting embrace. Until that moment I had held back my tears: telling myself that I must remain in control of my sorrow and this grievous situation: telling myself that I alone now stood at the helm, as my grandfather had once said; but now I could surrender command to my dear friend Sir Hedworth.

"There, there, my dear! No, do not try to stop weeping. It is best to let tears fall! Here, take my handkerchief!"

He held me close and I abandoned myself to the pent up grief and fear which had plagued me for so long: the strong arms that encircled me were a haven where I might find a little respite from the dreadful things which had been happening recently; and I wept until I could weep no more.

"Come, my dear, let us sit down and you can tell me what has passed. That is if you wish to speak of it, or would you rather seek your chamber?"

"I cannot say with any certainty what has taken place," I replied. "There was an explosion in Uncle James's laboratory. I was just returning from a ride when it happened, but what caused it I do not know. When they reached Uncle James he was dead, he had been suffocated by the smoke!"

"And Sylvia, where is she?" asked Sir Hedworth.

"Mrs Ambrose gave her something to make her sleep. She was prostrate with shock and grief!"

"Very wise, very wise. But where is Mrs Ambrose?"

"She is in her chamber."

"Her place is here with you, surely?"

"No, Sir Hedworth, I desired her to leave me."

"Lady Mary will arrive presently. We heard the sound of the explosion at Brett's Folly! Of course, we did not know what it was, but we knew that something must be amiss! I rode straight over here across the meadows, but it will take Lady Mary a little longer to come by the road. Now, my dear, you stay here whilst I go and see what is going on in the west wing. Has the doctor arrived yet?"

"Not to my knowledge," I answered. "I suppose he is taking his time. There is no reason for him to hasten!"

Oh, it is so good to have dear friends at hand in an hour of need! Gently, but firmly, Sir Hedworth took from my nerveless fingers the reins of Drawbridge Court.

"If you will not go to your room, stay here in the study," he instructed. "I shall keep you informed of all that takes place, but things of this nature are not to be dealt with by a young lady, however capable!"

Lady Mary arrived, and I wept afresh as I told her the little I knew of what had transpired; and she too wept, as we clung to each other in this hour of yet more tragedy. Uncle James had been like a brother to her: aggravating sometimes, amiable always, and very, very dear.

"You will stay with us at Brett's Folly for the time being," Lady Mary said.

"I should appreciate it if you will have my aunt and Mrs Ambrose to stay," I replied. "But my place is here! There are things to be done. Enquiries will be made into my uncle's death, and someone must be at hand! The house must be set to rights, as well!"

"Autumn, pray do not imagine for one moment that Sir Hedworth will allow you to undertake the unpleasant business which lies ahead. It is quite unthinkable that you should even consider it! Let us be sensible, my dear. You do not even know whom you should notify of this tragedy, and it is only right that you should not! We claim the privilege of old friends. I do not wish to appear high-handed, but in this I must insist that you be guided by Sir Hedworth and myself!"

My protests died on my lips: I could see the sense of what Lady Mary said, and I was indeed grateful. I dreaded the thought of the tumult which must ensue: once more the questions, the poking and prying: once more this dreadful day to be lived through again and again! The newspaper reporters would arrive hot-foot to waylay the servants: although an accidental death would not be so sensational as that which had befallen my beloved Grandpapa, it would make news! I could envisage the headlines, 'Wealthy Scientist Dies in Mysterious Explosion', and I thought of poor Uncle James lying upstairs. How eager and excited he had been at the prospect of his new discovery! For years and years he had worked, at last to be rewarded by recognition and perhaps even acclaim! He had striven so hard to reach his goal and when it was almost within sight it had been snatched away, together with his life!

The day after Uncle James's death we accepted the invitation of the Bretts. As Sir Hedworth said, Drawbridge Court was only a short distance away and I could drive over whenever I wished; and for the first time in my life I was able to leave my home with equanimity, nay relief! Until recently I had always regarded it as a place of peaceful serenity: a place where one was secure from worries and threats, but it was so no longer. In less than a year both Grandpapa and Uncle James had been taken from us: both of them had died violent and unnatural deaths, and it seemed as though the tranquillity with which the residents of Drawbridge Court had been blessed had come to an end.

Although the grief and shock I felt at Uncle James's death was painful enough to bear, that which was borne by my poor aunt was pitiful to witness. She and my uncle had never been a demonstrative couple; of course a show of affection in public would have been considered vulgar and in the worst of taste, but in their quiet way they had been utterly devoted to each other. Now, with no warning: no time in which to prepare and perhaps resign herself, her beloved husband had been taken from her! No more than a few minutes had passed from the time when she, Uncle James and Mrs Ambrose had been sitting together at breakfast; Aunt Sylvia gently teasing Uncle James to tell her of his invention and he smiling and trying to look firm, and equally as gently refusing her request.

"Patience, my love, patience!" he had said. "It will not be long now before I complete my work, and then you shall see!" and happily he had left the breakfast parlour not knowing he was going to his death!

There was the inquest and post-mortem: police once more inspected and examined and questioned: scientific experts came down from London to Drawbridge Court and poked about in what remained of Uncle James's sanctum to discover what they could, but when they emerged from the charred laboratory they were not much wiser than they had been before they descended the stone steps.

"Did they find out what caused the explosion?" I asked Sir Hedworth.

"They cannot be sure, my dear, but by all accounts it is a miracle that Drawbridge Court and all within it were not blown sky-high! I do not understand these matters but the experts tell me that they found traces of numerous elements, whatever they might be. Some were metallic and some non-metallic: some were harmless enough but others could be absolutely lethal if handled carelessly. The slightest mistake made when using things of that nature can cause untold damage and certain loss of life!"

"But Uncle James knew what he was about!" I protested. "He was well acquainted with things of that nature: he had worked with them for all of his adult life!"

"Nobody is infallible, Autumn. Just one moment of inattentiveness; one slip of the hand would have horrifying results, as indeed it has. I will tell you this, my dear: if I had known what was lodged in the cellars of the west wing, you would have found me a most reluctant visitor to your house. You were all living atop of what was virtually a keg of gun-powder!"

"I suppose it is possible that Uncle James made an error of judgement," I said. "But I find it very hard to accept that he did so. He was such a meticulous person!"

"In the usual way, yes, but I hear he was on the verge of completing some experiment on which he had been working. In his excitement, could he not have overlooked some precaution which he normally would have taken?"

"Not Uncle James, he was such a careful man!" I replied.

But was he? I had remarked the change in him when he had returned from London. He was excited certainly, and it was possible that Sir Hedworth's guess was correct.

"Did these experts discover aught of his invention?" I enquired. "Was there anything to indicate on what he had been working?"

"Alas, no. Most of James's papers had been burned: there were some which were saved, but their contents were either indecipherable or dealt with mundane matters. There was nothing to give even a hint of what had occupied your uncle these many years."

* * *

Dusk was falling as we laid Uncle James to rest beside Grandpapa in the family vault. We had chosen this time of day as the most unlikely to attract sensation seekers; and in the vault which had been opened twice in less than nine months after lying undisturbed for many years we said our final farewells to what remained of my kind, gentle, beloved uncle. Aunt Sylvia did not attend the interment: we had persuaded her to stay behind at Brett's Folly and when she went for her afternoon's rest I had without her knowledge instructed Miriam to double the amount of laudanum which Aunt Sylvia needed these days to enable her to sleep.

"When my aunt awakens we shall have returned from the church and it will all be over," I explained. "I do not want her to be here at Brett's Folly grieving and alone, when I am not within call!"

"Do you wish for me to remain here with Lady Kimberley, or accompany you to the church?" Mrs Ambrose asked.

"Well, as my aunt will be sleeping I would rather you came with me," I replied. "I shall be grateful for your support."

"I shall stay in her ladyship's dressing-room all the time you are away," Miriam offered.

"Thank you, Miriam. I know I can depend on you!"

And so it was done, and in the twilight we wended our sorrowing way back to Brett's Folly: grief was in my heart, and bitter regret that I had not appreciated fully the wonderful, happy life which we had been granted before tragedy struck not once, but twice. But there was room in my heart for something else as well: it was suspicion!

EIGHT

WE were still staying at Brett's Folly when Perry arrived: he had been abroad on a matter of business when Uncle James had met his death, but on his return to his estates in Derbyshire he had received a letter from Lady Mary telling him of the tragedy, and he had lost no time in coming to see if there was anything he could do to aid us.

Lord Peregrine Dexter and romance had been far from my thoughts lately, but when I saw him stride towards me quite unexpectedly as I sat in a small arbour in the gardens, I discovered that my love for him was as strong as ever. Nay, my love for him was stronger, deeper: it was the love of a woman for a man! The man! The only man who could fill her heart and life with joy! Gone were the superficial notions of capturing his admiration as I descended his stairs at Waring House, flaunting myself in a provocative gown of black lace: this love which I now bore him wanted only his happiness; and if happiness should come to him by wedding with another, so be it! Whatever he wanted, so I wanted for him; and if his desires did not march with mine, although I should endure a lifetime of loneliness, I was content.

He sat beside me and drew me close, and I rested my head upon his broad chest as though to do so was the most natural thing in the world: in the shelter of his powerful arms I felt like a little battered sailing vessel coming into safe harbour. It was so many years since I had felt the strength of those strong arms about me, and in their close embrace I felt all threats and worries were trivial things; nothing could harm me while he held me thus!

There was a light touch upon my head: whether he kissed my hair or rested his cheek upon it I do not know, but whichever it was brought bliss to my heart.

"I came as quickly as I could!" he murmured. "The moment I heard, I sped to your side. Oh my little love, I am so sorry! So sorry for the dreadful things which you have had to bear, and more sorry still that I was not here to help you in your time of need."

His nearness and the loving concern in his voice were my undoing: my hard-won self-control slipped from me, and I wept! Great racking sobs of grief and anguish: fear was there as well, and the growing suspicion that not every disaster had been an accident; and that there might even now be more horrors to come!

"Oh, I am s-s-so afraid!" I managed to stammer between my sobs.

"Afraid, my little queen? Tell me! Tell me of your fears!"

And so I did! To Perry I could pour out my heart. For the first time I could put into words the nagging doubts and dreadful suspicions which had plagued me since Grandpapa's death. Until that moment I had stood alone: the Bretts, though close friends, were not in my confidence for fear I should be thought an alarmist: Aunt Sylvia needed every reassurance to help her bear her grief, not the idea implanted in her mind that her husband might have been foully murdered, and that evil could still stalk amongst us! And Mrs Ambrose? Although sensible and of a sympathetic nature, she was still a servant in our employ; and one did not bare one's heart to servants!

Patiently Perry heard me out, just interrupting me occasionally to ask a relevant question when my tongue overtook my tale, so that some sense might be made of my disjointed outpourings. When I had finished he said gravely:

"Actually, apart from Sir Mark's violent death, nothing has taken place which could not be an accident! But added together, these incidents do seem to have been occurring too frequently to be pure chance!"

"But who could be responsible for them?" I asked. "And I have been followed! I know I have, I saw him! He was a thick-set man, dressed in brown and riding a bay!"

"He could have been anyone. I am more interested in this mysterious young man of whom you speak: the one who would not give you his name," Perry replied.

"Yes, it was strange! I told you I met him on the morning that Uncle James died, did I not? All the young man told me of himself was that he was exploring the district. But he was not staying with friends: he told me so!"

"I think I shall make enquiries regarding that young gentleman," Perry said. "He must have been staying at least overnight in an inn hereabouts, otherwise he would not have been on horseback in this vicinity so early in the morning!"

"Oh, it is all very mysterious and I am so glad you are here!" I gave a sigh of pure contentment; then I realized that I was still clasped to his bosom and, although I did not wish to, I felt the time had come to draw away and regain my composure. Intense joy flooded my entire being when I found that I could not! As I moved so the arms tightened their clasp, and in wonder I glanced up to the beloved face just above my own. The world stood still! Those cool, grey eyes so close to mine were no longer cool: they were warm with love and tenderness, and as I gazed into their depths the warmth in them was intensified, and the fire which I saw leap into them fanned my face to flame!

Like an eagle swooping upon his prey, so his lips captured mine: and oh, what a willing prey was I! With a kiss commanding yet gentle he conjured the soul from my body so that it went winging, close entwined with his, heavenwards! Passion swept through me: a passion such as I had never before known existed. My limbs were afire, and yet I was drowning: utterly helpless against the surging tide of emotions which swept through me, and the sensation was wonderful! My darling was initiating me into the first innocent joys of love-making: introducing me to the bliss and wonder of my first real kiss! At last his lips released my own and he strained me to him tightly, oh so tightly; and I rejoiced and marvelled that a man as strong as he should tremble so.

"Little queen," he whispered. "Will you be my wife? In the eyes of the world you would be my countess, but as queen you already reign in my heart."

For a terrible moment I found I could not speak: the magic of the moment had laid a spell upon my tongue and I could only gaze worshipfully into his eyes. No words of mine were eloquent enough to reveal the love which I bore him: had always borne him! Some mischievous fairy had robbed me of the power of speech and, dumb with ecstasy, I could only stare at him!

"Forgive me! I have startled you with my clumsiness! I am a brute to frighten you so!"

"No!"

Fool! Was I to lose him for want of a word?

"No? Is that your answer to my proposal of marriage?"

"No!" To make doubly sure he understood my meaning I shook my head as I uttered the word, then overcome by shyness I hid my face against his chest until he took my chin and tilted it upwards so I was forced to look at him.

"My darling, you are trembling! I must have alarmed you!" Perry whispered.

"Nay, my love, it is not fear that makes me tremble," I murmured, then amazed at my own daring I found that my hand had instinctively rested upon the back of my beloved's head to draw it closer to mine; and this time it was I who sought his lips!

Breathless and shaken we drew apart at last and Perry gazed at me with amazement.

"Whoever would believe it?" he said with wonder in his voice. "I can recall, oh so clearly, a small maiden stomping towards me on her chubby little legs. Along this very path she would come, imperious in her demands to be set upon my shoulder. Now her rightful place is in my heart! Am I permitted to observe that the chubbiness seems to have disappeared, to be replaced by the most delightful contours imaginable!"

Hurriedly I glanced down, and blushed to the roots of my hair! As my darling and I had embraced, my gown had somehow become strained against me so that my form was clearly outlined, and my lower limbs might have had no covering at all as from hip to ankle their shape was all too evident to the admiring gaze of my loved one. As I made to rise he held me even more firmly and laughed down into my confused countenance.

"Let me go! Someone might come!" I pleaded.

"Very well," he agreed reluctantly. "Those enchantments are for my eyes alone, or will be as soon as I can make them so. There! You have righted your gown, now come and sit beside me."

I needed no second bidding, and nestled close against him while we made our plans for the wonderful future which would be ours.

"As soon as we return to the house we shall announce our betrothal," Perry said firmly.

"No, we cannot do that!" I objected. "I am in mourning, and will be for another year!"

"We shall make an informal announcement immediately. I want to shout it from the roof-tops, but I agree that we must show a proper respect for your uncle and grandsire. Our families are not dim-witted. If we do not tell them, they will guess our secret. They have only to look at us!"

But the vexed question of whether or not to proclaim to our immediate relatives our love and intentions was decided for us. As we sat, completely engrossed in the wonder of each other's company, we were discovered.

"Autumn? Peregrine? Are you there?" and before we had time to move apart to present a more circumspect appearance, around a bend in the path came Aunt Sylvia, Lady Mary, and Mrs Ambrose. With an arm still about my shoulders Perry rose to his feet, drawing me with him, and side by side we waited for the three ladies to reach us.

"Ladies, you are the first to hear our news, and I hope to wish us joy. Autumn has just made me the happiest man alive by consenting to become my wife!"

* * *

To have the man whom I had worshipped all my

life return my love was a wondrous thing, but how much more joyous I should have felt if Grandpapa and Uncle James had lived to give us their blessing and wish us well upon our betrothal. Poor Aunt Sylvia tried so hard to overcome her grief: bravely she smiled as she bade my beloved and me:

"Bend your heads you great creatures, so that I may kiss you! Autumn is dearer to me than any daughter and it rejoices my soul that now I am to have one whom I can call son-in-law, and that the gentleman of her choice should be you, Peregrine! May God bless you both as I do, and grant that you may enjoy many happy years together."

As the days passed I grew increasingly worried about my aunt. When in company she tried to put her sorrow behind her, but sometimes when she thought she was alone the stricken expression upon her dear face was enough to rend the heart. Most mornings her eyes were red-rimmed with weeping, and she began to lose weight at an alarming rate. Gowns which had once fitted her little plump form all too snugly, now needed to be taken in at the seams!

There was another matter which gave me cause for concern. Although the Bretts were kindness itself and assured us of a welcome for as long as we should choose to remain beneath their roof, we could not accept their hospitality for ever! It was time that we took our leave of them, but whenever I mentioned the subject of returning home to my aunt she put me off with this excuse or that, until I realized that she had conceived a dread of once more taking up residence at Drawbridge Court. Her feelings were completely understandable. I had driven across to my home several times since the death of Uncle James: the broken windows had all been re-glazed and the house set to rights, but still one could smell the acrid reek of smoke and fumes in the atmosphere and this would be a constant reminder to Aunt Sylvia of the day when she had been widowed in such a dreadful fashion. Time would erase this last lingering trace, I knew, but what was to be done until then?

"I do not know what to do for the best," I told Mrs Ambrose one day. She and I were strolling in the gardens of Brett's Folly whilst Aunt Sylvia was resting: although it was November the weather was unseasonably mild and some of the flowerbeds were still bright with bloom.

She was thoughtful for a few moments and then replied:

"Well, there is only one answer so far as I can see. That is to spend the next few months away from here, in a place that is completely different! Oh, I do not mean abroad: that would be asking too much of Lady Kimberley's health at the moment. No: I think a visit to some quiet seaside resort would be beneficial not only to your aunt's health, but to your own as well, Miss Kimberley."

"Mine? Oh, I am well enough, I assure you."

"You may think so, my dear, but pray allow me to speak my mind. I have known you for just over a year and in that short time you have suffered shocks, bereavement, and a near fatal accident. You have accepted responsibilities which would make many an older person think twice before undertaking them, and now recently you have become betrothed. So many things have happened to you that it would be a wonder if your health had not suffered in some way or another, and though I know that this is an unpleasant truth I will say it! You would easily pass for a woman five years your senior, instead of a young person only just twenty!"

"Mrs Ambrose, those words are most unflattering!" I

smiled. "Could you not have said that I have matured rather too quickly?"

"I could, but to play the part of friend I fear I must shock you into the realization of the true state of affairs. Through every crisis you have remained calm: others have turned to you for instruction, and I admire the way in which you have controlled your feelings and the manner in which you have behaved. But every person has a breaking point! Miss Kimberley, you are too thin, too pale, there are circles under your eyes and you have developed a tendency to glance over your shoulder for no apparent reason! There, I have said it! If I offend you I am sorry, but I stand by what I say!"

"No, I am not offended," I replied slowly. "I am grateful that you should care sufficiently for my welfare to tell me the truth as you see it."

"Well, then, will you consider what I have suggested? You must think of yourself not only for your aunt's sake, but for the sake of your fiancé. What would either of them do if you should become ill? And another thing!" She smiled. "Do you not think that Lord Dexter would prefer his bride to be radiant and blooming rather than peeked and wan? Where is your vanity, my dear? Do you not wish to be known as the beautiful Countess of Waring?"

Mrs Ambrose had me laughing for the first time in weeks.

"I have only one objection to make to this idea of yours," I said. "Winter will soon be upon us! It would be far too cold at a coastal resort at this time of year for my aunt!"

"Not so, Miss Kimberley. A friend of my last employers always wintered at Broadstairs. It is a quiet town favoured by those in delicate health who have no wish to travel abroad and so avoid the rigours of the coldest months. The climate is exceptionally mild there, and the sea breezes are so good for one's health! I should think that Lady Kimberley would like it very much. She could meet genteel people there if she chose, and so perhaps be able to recover a little from her grief!"

"Well, I could ask my aunt if she would like to go," I said.

"If you could persuade her to agree, it would be the very thing for both of you," Mrs Ambrose continued. "Whilst we are here or at Drawbridge Court, Lady Kimberley has not enough to occupy her waking hours. She has too much time for thought and regrets. A change of scene, new faces about her, and a winter in Broadstairs where the mild weather would enable her to enjoy short walks and drives would be of such benefit to her! If she will not go, I dread to think what the coming season spent at Drawbridge Court will bring. We might be house-bound for weeks, and can you imagine how melancholy Lady Kimberley would become then?"

I could indeed, and resolved at that moment that we should not return to Drawbridge Court for at least three months. If Aunt Sylvia would not go to Broadstairs, then we must find somewhere else to stay for the coming winter. Christmas was approaching apace, and it would be too heart-rending to spend it at our home where only the year before Grandpapa had taken his place at the head of the table, and Uncle James had sat and smiled benignly upon us all. No: it would be too sad to even contemplate!

But Aunt Sylvia did not demure when the suggestion was put to her that we visit the sea before eventually returning to Drawbridge Court. She did not sound eager either, but the poor soul seemed to have lost interest in everything, so her lack of it did not give me cause to reconsider the plan which had been put forward by Mrs Ambrose.

"Yes, dear, that sounds as if it will be most pleasant," Aunt Sylvia said, so I went ahead with making the arrangements. Actually, I did not arrange anything; I left all in the hands of Mr Dawson, our solicitor, who was his usual, helpful self. Lady Mary and Sir Hedworth voiced their approval when told of our intentions and my darling Perry promised that he would come and spend Christmas with us at Broadstairs.

"I must return to Derbyshire on estate matters," he told me. "But I shall join you before Christmas, and will stay for as long as I am able. My business will not take me more than a week or so to complete. I will not dally over it. Every day I do not see you, is a day lost. Oh, my beloved, never again will a year be so long as this one which I must wait before you become my bride!"

* * *

In less than three weeks we set off for Broadstairs. Mr Dawson had experienced no difficulty in hiring a house for us, together with the necessary staff who would see to our needs and comfort; and Sir Hedworth had very kindly taken it upon himself to ensure that we had a smooth journey thither. For the first time since her bereavement, Aunt Sylvia had been persuaded to take an active part in something. I should say forced rather than persuaded, and though I had to steel myself to do it, I knew that I must!

"Aunt Sylvia, you will have to make out a list of the things which you wish to take to Broadstairs with you," I informed her. "Miriam must have some guide from which to work, otherwise you will find yourself with nothing suitable to wear upon our arrival."

"Oh, I am sure that there is no need for me to do so, Autumn. Miriam will know what I wish to pack. She is such a sensible creature!"

"Perhaps she is, but it would hardly be fair to expect her to fill your trunks with no list to aid her. Most of your warmer garments are at Drawbridge Court, as you know. Of course, if you choose to go over there yourself to supervise the packing there will be no problem," I said relentlessly.

Poor Aunt Sylvia winced at the suggestion and decided to make the best of a bad bargain.

"Very well, dear. I will ask Mrs Ambrose to help me make out my list."

* * *

My aunt, Mrs Ambrose and I, together with Miriam and Rose and, of course, Carlin, all shared the railway compartments reserved for us by Sir Hedworth; although for the drives to and from the railway stations we did have separate carriages from the servants. The heavy luggage had been sent ahead, and I was grateful to Mrs Ambrose for the way in which she took charge of our small party in the most efficient yet unobtrusive manner imaginable.

The house in which we should stay was in Pierremont Avenue, and as soon as I saw it I was delighted with Mr Dawson's selection. It was double-fronted but not too large, having only six principal bedchambers; and it looked as though it was an older building than its neighbours. Although not so smart and fashionable as they, our house gave the appearance of solid comfort; its red brick walls mellowed by time, and adorned with the glowing leaves of a creeper which must have been planted when the house was young.

At the head of the staff were Mrs Rose, the housekeeper, and Rose, her husband, who was butler. Then there were Cook, three maidservants, a footman, and a youth who made himself useful generally. They were all standing in line as we entered the hall and they made their obeisances in a most respectful manner; although when we smiled at them as they were presented to us, they returned our smiles and I thought I could discern a look of relief on more than one face.

Mrs Rose conducted us over the house, remarking as she did so:

"Fires have been lit in all the bedchambers, my lady: each one is ready for immediate occupation. Not knowing which chambers you ladies would select I judged it best to ready them all, so that if you should desire to rest immediately there need be no last-minute preparation."

"That was most thoughtful of you, Mrs Rose," my aunt replied. "I can see that the house is in the charge of an extremely capable person, and I must say it is quite a relief to find it so."

Mrs Rose looked gratified.

"You are most kind to say so, my lady," she said, then, "From these chambers the outlook is most pleasant, ma'am. Those are the grounds of Pierremont Hall. You can catch a glimpse of the rooftops of the mansion over yonder. Her Majesty spent several summers there when she was a young maiden."

"Indeed? How interesting!" Aunt Sylvia exclaimed. "We shall rely upon you, Mrs Rose, to tell us of other places of interest in this vicinity for when we plan our excursions."

"It will be a pleasure, ma'am."

"I think I will have this chamber," my aunt announced. "Which one have you chosen, Autumn?"

But my reply was not immediately forthcoming, for at that moment pandemonium broke loose. Carlin had been as good as gold the whole journey through, but now that we had arrived at our destination I had released him from his leash and he had pattered behind us from room to room exploring this, his new territory. His territory, and he was not the dog to suffer intruders, especially those in the shape of a large fat tabby cat! With a joyous bark he set off in pursuit of the animal; his paws slipping and slithering on the polished floorboards, rugs scattering in all directions and fragile pieces of furniture bearing ornamental pots and vases swaying perilously as quarry and hunter raced along corridors and into and out of chambers.

"Stop them, somebody!" I cried, but the appeal was futile. The hunt was on, and no lumbering two-footed creature was swift enough to stop the headlong flight. It only came to an end when the cat sprang to safety on top of a wardrobe; to swear and spit at its tormentor who, quivering with excitement, was hurling challenges from the floor below.

"Is the cat yours, Mrs Rose?" I asked the housekeeper.

"Yes, Miss Kimberley."

"Oh dear, I am so sorry! He has come to no harm, but I would not have released my dog if I had known that there was a cat here. I am afraid that Carlin is not used to seeing them in the house!"

"It is I who am sorry, Miss. Tiger has no business to be in this part of the house at all! He is only allowed below stairs, whether there are residents here or not. If you will allow me to, Miss Kimberley, I will get him down from the wardrobe and take him away to where he belongs."

"I do hope that there will not be any trouble if he and Carlin meet again," I said.

"Well, if they should, I doubt if they will do any more than they have just done, Miss Kimberley," Mrs Rose replied, then turned to her cat. "There, Tiger, that should teach you your place!"

"You are a bad dog, Carlin," I scolded, but he wagged his curly tail unrepentantly and gazed with longing in his eyes at the by now retreating form of Mrs Rose who had the cat safely cradled in her arms.

"We are off to a fine start!" remarked Mrs Ambrose, laughing. "Shall we retire to our chambers whilst peace reigns, or do you think we should descend for tea?"

"I think I shall rest now, but tea would be nice. I know, I shall ring for a tray," said my aunt.

"An excellent notion," I agreed. "I shall do the same, and I advise you to as well, Mrs Ambrose. Shall we meet downstairs for dinner?"

And so it was arranged.

* * *

The next few days passed pleasantly enough. We explored the town and found a goodly assortment of shops in the High Street: we walked along the sea-front and watched the little fishing boats returning and departing from the shelter of the pier: we sauntered along Albion Street hoping to catch a glimpse of the popular writer, Mr Dickens, who had been known to stay in the hotel there, but of course we were disappointed; and on our first Sunday in Broadstairs we hired a carriage to take us to the Church of the Holy Trinity so that we might worship our Maker.

It was whilst we were emerging from there that I glanced up suddenly, to stare into the face of Luker! Could it be he? If it were not, then the man was his double! But Luker was at Drawbridge Court, attending to his duties as footman: no, it could not be he, but the first sight of the man gave me quite a start! Of course, it was just my imagination at work: it was foolish to be so concerned over such a trivial coincidence.

When Mrs Ambrose had drawn my attention to the fact that I glanced over my shoulder more often than was needful, I had thought she had been exaggerating somewhat; but now that I was aware of this newly-formed habit of mine, I discovered she had spoken the truth! During the days immediately preceding Uncle James's death I had suspected I was being followed, but since then the feeling had left me until our arrival in Broadstairs. Yes: I did glance frequently over my shoulder, and several times I caught sight of the man whom I had taken to be Luker when first I spied him. Was it he, or was it the fact that I had felt uneasy about him when he had entered our employ at Drawbridge Court, that caused the image of the man to haunt me so?

But who was the middle-aged gentleman in brown? Why should he appear so often in our wake when we went walking? On the morning of Uncle James's death I had thought that there was a horseman dressed in brown pursuing me! Could these two men be the same one? What a stupid fancy! Just because a gentleman chose to be clad in brown, it did not mean that he wished me harm! It was the association of ideas, that was all: if there had been a pursuer he would surely have more than one coat to his back, and could be clothed in raiment of any colour! My overwrought nerves were making me ridiculously suspicious: Mrs Ambrose had been quite right! I had not realized before just how frayed they had become and I resolved to master my fears, and to take myself in hand. But all the same, I did wish that the middle-aged gentleman clad in brown would find somewhere else to take himself than in our train when we went strolling!

For the first week of our stay the weather remained fine. We were able to venture forth every day and soon were on nodding terms with other ladies whom we saw in the circulating library, and with our immediate neighbours in Pierremont Avenue. I observed with great satisfaction that my aunt's appetite was beginning to improve slightly, and that a little more colour was appearing in her cheeks.

"Mrs Ambrose, I am so thankful that you suggested we should come here," I told her when my aunt was absent from the room one afternoon. "Aunt Sylvia is improving daily!"

"Yes, I too have noticed that not only her health but her spirits as well seem to have benefited from this change of scene," Mrs Ambrose agreed. "Broadstairs is just as it was described to me, but it is a pity that the Assembly Rooms are closed for the winter. I know that neither you nor Lady Kimberley would wish to attend the Balls which are held there during the summer, but a concert or recital would be quite acceptable as entertainment even when one is in mourning!"

"Somewhere to go occasionally during the evenings would be nice," I replied. "Now that it is growing dark so early, the time after dinner is the most difficult to fill. But never mind, if we were at home we would have to be content with our own amusements and each other's company. We are no worse off than if we were there!"

All was well until it started to rain! Mrs Ambrose had been proved quite correct in her statement that the town enjoyed a mild climate: indeed, after the rain started the atmosphere remained mild, but clammy; whereas I should have preferred more seasonable weather as Christmas approached. I would have welcomed frost, or even snow: with either we could have left the house to enjoy a little exercise; but the steadily falling rain meant that we were house-bound. We all became bored, and I had to watch Carlin carefully: he, as bored as we, was constantly attempting to sneak off kitchenwards to seek the only diversion which was available to him, the persecution of Mrs Rose's cat!

Even though we should be absent from Drawbridge Court for Christmas I had done my best to arrange that the staff there should not suffer because of this. I had written to Mrs Wilkes charging her to see that the festive board was as it was normally: of course, as my home was a house of mourning there would be no unseemly jollity, but apart from all that all was to be the same as every other year. Upon my instruction Mrs Wilkes was to send the first of the Christmas wagon-loads of comforts to St Martin's in Rochester; and Mr Biggs, my agent, was to make sure that all of my tenants had their usual Yuletide benefits.

The three days during which the rain descended seemed like an eternity, but on the fourth a fitful sun filtered through the clouds, a fresh breeze arose, and I had a letter from my beloved! He would be with us in two days' time! He had bespoken rooms at the Albany Hotel and could stay for at least a fortnight, possibly longer! The vexing question of the weather paled into the veriest insignificance: it could rain, snow, hail or blow for all I cared. In two days' time I should see my darling, and all I had to do until then was count the hours!

NINE

ONE more day must be lived through before I should see my fiancé. I was determined to look to the glorious future which lay ahead of us, instead of dwelling upon the recent tragic past. What was done was done, and no amount of conjecture or suspicion could bring the two dearly-loved members of my family back to us. Life must go on, but things seemed to have started to improve at last! Aunt Sylvia was beginning to look a little more like her former self: although some mornings there were signs of tears shed during the night upon her dear face, the stricken look was fading and occasionally we managed to make her even laugh!

"It will be so nice to see Peregrine again!" she remarked as we sat at breakfast. "I suppose he will break his journey from Derbyshire, and spend the night at Brett's Folly."

"He did not say," I replied. "I expect you are right. It would be a sensible thing for him to do."

"I hope he does," Aunt Sylvia said. "For then he will be sure to bring messages from Lady Mary and Sir Hedworth. How fortunate it is that the rain had ceased at last! If it remains fine, perhaps we can enjoy some of the drives into the surrounding district which we promised ourselves when we arrived!"

But that morning we contented our need for exercise with a short walk to the High Street and its immediate vicinity, there to purchase some little gifts for the staff of our temporary residence, who were serving us so well. It was just after luncheon that my aunt complained of a slight headache.

"I think I shall retire to my chamber for the afternoon," she announced. "If I take some of my drops and sleep for a short while, it will probably be gone when I awaken. But do not stay indoors on my account, I beg of you. I shall not come down until it is time for dinner, so I will not miss your company if you choose to take advantage of the sunshine and venture forth."

Aunt Sylvia left us shortly afterwards, and I turned to Mrs Ambrose.

"What shall we do?" I enquired.

"I am entirely at your disposal, Miss Kimberley," she replied. "But if you wish to know what I should like to do, I shall answer you by saying that I would enjoy a really tiring walk. After being cooped up in the house for the last few days it would be a shame to waste a lovely afternoon like this!"

The idea appealed to me, and I asked:

"Have you anywhere in mind?"

"Yes, as a matter of fact I have. What do you say to a walk along the cliff-tops? From what I have heard the path may be a trifle rugged, but you and I are both agile people. I think it might be too difficult for Lady Kimberley to attempt; but whilst she is resting for the afternoon, we have the opportunity to see for ourselves if the view from there is as remarkable as the local people say!"

"That does sound much more attractive than our usual stroll around the streets of Broadstairs," I agreed. "Which way shall we go?"

"Well, if we set out westwards and the walk does not prove too tiring, we could go as far as Ramsgate. I believe it is only just over two miles away along the cliff path."

"Two miles? I thought you said you wanted a really tiring excursion," I remarked. "Oh, I see what you mean! It would be four miles if we walked there and back again!"

"I think if we reach the town of Ramsgate we can congratulate ourselves on our achievement in doing so," Mrs Ambrose smiled. "The path could be difficult, and may entail any amount of ascent and descent. When and if we reach our destination we could have tea, and then hire a carriage to drive us back to Broadstairs."

"Shall I bring Carlin?" I asked.

"Do you think his little legs could manage the trip we plan to undertake? I have my doubts on that score! If you do bring him, it is more than likely that we shall be carrying him before we are halfway there!"

"Yes, that is true."

At that moment the footman entered the room to mend the fire, and as he was a local man he was able to direct us to the nearest way to the west cliffs. When he heard of our intention to hire a carriage to bring us back he suggested:

"I could send one from the carriage-rank nearby to meet you ladies at Ramsgate. That would save you the trouble of hiring a vehicle when you get there!"

"Yes, Wilfred, it would," Mrs Ambrose replied. "But we should have to find it, and as we are strangers to Ramsgate I think it would be easier for us to locate a carriage-rank, than a single carriage! Anyone will direct us to a place from where we can hire a conveyance!"

"You are right, ma'am," Wilfred answered. "But I pray you, do take care! It is unwise to venture too near the edge of the cliffs, especially after all the rain that has fallen. The cliffs have been known to crumble, and if the path is muddy it will be slippery as well!"

"Thank you for your warning," I said. "Yes, we will take care."

"And I should wear a heavy cloak if I were you, Miss. The breeze will be much stronger up there than it is here in the town!"

"If we do not start soon, it will be dark before we leave the house!" interposed Mrs Ambrose. "Let us make ready and set out!"

It was just after two o'clock when Mrs Ambrose and I reached the path which would lead us along the top of the cliffs, and so to Ramsgate. We stood and gazed in awe at the panoramic view spread before us. As Wilfred had predicted, the breeze was strong; indeed, it was more than a breeze! It whipped white crests on the waves as they gradually covered the sea-weed-strewn rocks far below us, pinned our skirts against our limbs and caused our cloaks to stream out behind us until we fastened them securely from throat to hem. The sun was no longer shining, so I said as we contemplated the grey sky above:

"We shall become chilled if we stand here for long! Do you think it is likely to rain again?"

"Oh, no, I am convinced it will not. The sun will appear again presently, I am sure. Look, that must be the coast of France over there!"

My gaze followed the direction of Mrs Ambrose's pointing finger to see a blur upon the horizon.

"Do you see?" she enquired.

"Yes, I do. I also see those clouds which are gathering atop of it!" I replied. "This wind is blowing them straight in our direction!"

"Well, they are a long way away and if it does, it will probably blow them over our heads and on to some luckless place inland. This breeze is bringing a fine colour to your cheeks, Miss Kimberley. By the time we reach Ramsgate you will be positively glowing!"

"I expect I shall!" I answered. "I apply your prophecy to the saying, 'Horses sweat, gentlemen perspire, and ladies glow!' and by the look of the incline immediately before us, we shall both be glowing long before we reach Ramsgate!"

Once we had started, I found that I was enjoying our walk immensely. We kept well away from the actual edge of the cliff but the path was only muddy where it was shielded from the strong wind blown in from the sea. There was springy turf at either side of it so we were able to walk side by side, except where we aided each other over the difficult places; but as Mrs Ambrose had said, neither my aunt nor my little dog would have been able to undertake the walk without assistance. Carlin had pleaded to be allowed to accompany us, but I had been firm in ignoring his whimpers and now had cause to be thankful that I had done so.

We were less than halfway to Ramsgate when certain muscles which hitherto I had not even known I possessed began to make their presence felt, and when we crested a particularly steep rise I gasped to my companion:

"Pray, let us stop for a moment or two and catch our breath."

"Certainly, Miss Kimberley. The way has been a trifle difficult, has it not? Let us pause awhile and admire the prospect before us."

A trifle difficult, indeed! Then I looked at Mrs Ambrose and was filled with admiration for this lady who must be twice my age. Her eyes were sparkling and her colour was high, but she seemed no whit distressed by the arduous walk which we had only half accomplished; whereas I was gasping like a landed fish! I was tall, but Mrs Ambrose was taller, and she was built on Junoesque proportions so that I should have thought her movements across country such as this would be cumbersome. Not so: she trod lightly and surefootedly, and as my eyes rested on the footprints we had just made I realized that she was wearing far more sensible footwear than I was. My walking boots had only a heel of medium height, but those of Mrs Ambrose seemed to be completely flat: more like a man's than a woman's! For the first time I noticed what large feet the lady had: those of peasant stock, Grandpapa would have said! Some low-born ancestor of Mrs Ambrose must be held responsible for their size; and she, poor lady, must go through life with them!

"Well, Miss Kimberley, we have not been drenched by rain," Mrs Ambrose observed.

"Not yet, but we are still quite a distance from our destination," I replied.

"Shall we proceed upon our way, then?"

"Just give me a moment more. Really, Mrs Ambrose, you put me to shame! There you stand as calm and unruffled as can be, whereas I am only just recovering my breath!"

She smiled. "Actually, I am rather pleased with myself. It is a long while since I covered any great distance on foot."

We stood looking about us for a little while longer and suddenly I shivered. The south-east wind had veered to the east, bringing with it a definite chill. Not only that, it had, as I had predicted, brought the clouds which I had remarked upon earlier. They were massing overhead with no break in them for as far as the eye could see: indeed, those furthest away were almost black! Seagulls wheeled and circled above us uttering their mournful cries, and as I stood there with Mrs Ambrose and no other living soul in sight a feeling of unease came over me.

"I am ready to resume our walk now," I said. "Will you go first?"

The path had narrowed somewhat with bramble bushes upon the landward side of it so it was necessary to walk in single file, but for some strange reason I did not care to have my companion walking behind me!

"Certainly, Miss Kimberley. Shall we put up our hoods before we start? If it should rain, doing so will protect our bonnets a little."

Mrs Ambrose was wearing one which was rather distinctive: it was of dark blue velvet, with two white silk roses as ornamentation. Privately, I thought the style a trifle juvenile for a lady of her mature years to wear; but she obviously liked it as she wore it so often, and her choice of head-gear was nothing to do with me! I raised the hood of my cloak and nodded to indicate that I was ready, and we continued on our way.

The feeling of relief which flooded through me when I spied a gentleman at the top of the next rise was ridiculous.

"Look yonder, Mrs Ambrose," I said. "We are not the only intrepid wayfarers abroad on the cliffs this afternoon!"

She did not reply and I assumed that the wind had carried the words from my lips. The gentleman did not approach us nor precede us along the cliff path; he just stood staring out to sea, and I glanced in the same direction as he to see if there was anything interesting to hold his attention so. But no; there was nothing but the white-crested waves, the black lowering clouds, and the circling seagulls.

As we neared the spot where the gentleman was standing he turned to face us, and for the moment I felt overcome with astonishment at the sheer coincidence of our meeting. It was the stranger who had rescued me when my mare had bolted upon the morning of Uncle James's death! The smile of recognition froze on my face as I heard him say to Mrs Ambrose:

"About time, too! I have been up here every afternoon when it wasn't raining for the last ten days! Where the devil have you been?"

"Miss Kimberley found the walk a trifle tiring," she replied. "Pray, permit me to present my son to you, Miss Kimberley."

"Your son, Mrs Ambrose? I had no idea you had one! How do you do, sir? I am happy to make your acquaintance."

"I am honoured, ma'am," he replied, then he laughed. "Come, enough of this charade. We cannot do our business here for another two hours: the tide will not be in until then. But we must get off this path! Someone might come along!"

Was the poor young man deranged? Was this the reason why his mother never spoke of him: did she try to keep from the world the knowledge that her son was not quite so sane as he should be? Was he kept hidden away for fear that he should embarrass her by his ravings? If so, I felt sorry for the young man! Simple he might be, but he was harmless, surely? But what were ravings to me made sense to his mother. She was frowning as though to hush him, but enquired:

"You have found somewhere near?"

"Of course. Not too near though. If you will follow me, I will lead you to it."

I stared in blank bewilderment from one to the other until Mrs Ambrose turned to address me.

"You are right, Miss Kimberley. I am sure it is going to rain again. If you will be so kind as to follow my son, he will lead us to shelter. I shall walk behind you."

"I do not think that would be wise, Mrs Ambrose," I objected. "If the heavens do open once more, the rain will not cease till long after nightfall. Look at the sky! It is almost as black as pitch! No; our best course is to make all speed to Ramsgate."

But her fingers closed on my upper arm in a vice-like grip, and she hissed in a voice completely different from any I had heard her use before:

"Do as you are bid! Bernard, come and help me with her. We must not dally here!"

"How dare you manhandle me?" I demanded indignantly. "Release me at once!" and I struggled to free myself from her grasp. Although she was far stronger than I, my efforts were nearly successful until her son came to her aid.

"Be still!" he grated between his teeth. "Be still, or I shall clout you into submission!"

Then with one hand holding me firmly by the elbow and the other like a clamp at the back of my neck, he thrust me ahead of him as we left the cliff path and began to travel inland.

"What are you doing? Where are you taking me?" I cried as I was borne along. There was no other soul in sight but we three: nobody to lend an ear to my shouts for help, or to aid me in my distress. It was impossible to match my pace to his: he took great strides and I slipped and stumbled and several times fell; but each time I did so he hauled me to my feet to push me ahead once more as we continued our flight, from what I knew not.

The coarse turf which covered the cliff-tops gave way to meadow-land, one of which we crossed: then somehow we scrambled through a hedge into a coppice, traversed that, and before us was the ruin of a small stone building of some sort.

"Here we are! In with you," and with a mighty shove I was sent hurtling through a doorway and across what had once been a ground floor room; to fall headlong at the other side of it and lie there shaking with shock and fighting to regain my breath.

Mrs Ambrose regarded me closely, then having obviously decided that I was *hors de combat* she turned her attention to her son and asked:

"You have brought everything? All is arranged?"

"Yes, Ma. The horses are tethered at the back, and your stuff is over yonder."

Without giving me another glance Mrs Ambrose crossed to where was standing a canvas bag: she opened the drawstring at the neck of it, peered inside, nodded with satisfaction, and before my astonished eyes proceeded to disrobe! Was she as mad as her son? In dreadful fascination I watched as she removed her cloak and bonnet, skirt and jacket, to stand before us in shirt, riding breeches, and boots. Men's riding boots! Then from the bag she drew a gentleman's tail-coat, a man's riding coat with capes, and a curly brimmed top hat. These garments she proceeded to don until she was standing before us clad as a man: and indeed with her height and breadth of shoulder she would easily pass for one. Then she turned to me and laughed.

"How the mighty are fallen, Miss Kimberley," she said. "You may sit up. We have a little wait ahead of us."

"Are you both out of your senses?" I demanded. "What on earth do you think you are doing?"

"We do not think: we know! Bernard, go and make sure that all is well with the horses. And make sure that there is nobody about, either. We cannot afford anything to go wrong now!"

"The horses? Are you seriously planning to abduct me and hold me for ransom?" I asked angrily. "You must be out of your minds if you think you can succeed in such an undertaking! My fiancé will not rest until you are caught. He will hound you for the rest of your lives!"

"Ah, the great Lord Dexter! His enquiries will prove fruitless. Oh, no doubt he will make them, but abduction is not what we have in mind for you, Miss High-and-Mighty. No, we plan something very different!"

"You speak as though I have injured you in some way." I felt anger leave me and fear begin to take its place. "I have always treated you fairly. You cannot hate me enough to harm me, and you have nothing to gain by doing so."

"So, even now you suspect nothing? I am very pleased to hear it. If you cannot guess even now, neither will anyone else, ever! You wish to know what we will gain? Well, I will tell you: there is plenty of time in which to do so. We will gain far more than a paltry ransom and the risk which it would bring. We shall gain your inheritance, Autumn Kimberley: we shall gain every acre and penny you own!"

"You are mad!" My suspicion was now a certainty but my peril was as great, if not greater than I had feared. What did these two maniacs plan for me?

"If it pleases you to think so, you may," Mrs Ambrose smiled down at me. "Actually, we are extremely clever. So clever that I cannot resist the temptation to tell you of our cleverness. The initial idea was mine, but my son has been so helpful that he deserves his share of admiration."

If I could keep her talking and convince her that she had my full attention as she narrated her mad tale, I could perhaps make a dash for the doorway. Bernard had gone to ascertain that the horses were ready, and if I could take Mrs Ambrose unawares I might yet escape from this lunatic pair. Once I was free of these four walls terror would lend wings to my heels, and before I was overtaken I might find someone to succour me.

"For over a year I have taken your orders, and those of your pampered aunt," Mrs Ambrose continued. "Yes, my lady: no, my lady! Yes, Miss Kimberley; certainly, Miss Kimberley! But soon I shall be the mistress giving the orders, and others will run to do my bidding! Oh, not the mistress of Drawbridge Court: that would be too dangerous! We shall sell that damned old place and with the money purchase something equally as grand and far more modern. We plan to settle in Italy."

"Yes, that would be a wise thing to do, Mrs Ambrose," I agreed, to humour her.

"I am so pleased you approve of our decision," she replied. "You may be able to understand the situation in which you find yourself if I suggest that you call me Aunt Helen! When you have gone to join your pompous grandsire and your useless uncle, which will be very shortly, after a decent interval my son can claim his inheritance. Your inheritance, Autumn Kimberley! Yes, he is your cousin and I am your aunt!"

"What are you saying?" I whispered.

"I am telling you that I am as much your aunt as that coddled creature whom you call Aunt Sylvia. I am telling you that the time has now come for my son and myself to enjoy our share of the Kimberley wealth! I am the widow of your Uncle Harold, and Bernard is his true son and heir! I say heir, but it was not until my husband died that I discovered that there might be anything to inherit. Certainly he left nothing but a pile of debts and a shameful memory."

"I do not believe you!" I faltered, but in my heart I knew she was speaking the truth.

"That scarcely matters, my dear. I do not have the time to prove the truth of my words to you: all must be accomplished this afternoon."

"What do you mean?"

"There is no reason why you should not know. I shall tell you: it will help to pass the time until we leave this place. In just over an hour we shall retrace our steps, then once we reach the cliff-tops, over you will go! This cloak and bonnet which I have discarded will follow you, and tomorrow all of Broadstairs will be horrified to learn of the fate of two ladies who went walking along the cliff path, to slip and fall to their deaths upon the rocks below! Your body will be washed ashore; my poor remains will never be found, but my bonnet and cloak will tell their own sad story. Once the third tragedy in the luckless family of Kimberley has been accomplished my son and I will return here, mount our horses and ride away, and Mrs Ambrose will never be seen or heard of again!"

"You will murder me?" I whispered incredulously. "You intend to kill me just for the sake of money?"

"That is reason enough," was the cool reply. "You may speak of money with contempt, but you have never been without it, have you? You have never felt the pangs of hunger grip your belly, not heard your child cry himself to sleep because he cannot understand why there is no supper! You have never been hounded from place to place, dodging creditors; not worn your fingers to the bone taking in other people's laundry, to have a few pitful coppers you have earned taken from you by a husband who thought he was too fine to work for them himself, so that he might gamble them away!"

"Surely there was no need for that!" I protested. "He had only to appeal to my grandfather for financial help! Anyone can find themselves in temporary difficulties!"

"Temporary? You make me smile! There was a very good reason why he did not appeal to Sir Mark for funds, and that was because he was packed off to Australia in disgrace for cheating at cards. Oh, it was all hushed up of course but he told me all about it, protesting his innocence and I believed him at the time: but that was how he came to his death! He chose the wrong man to cheat, and was fatally shot over the card-table in a dirty, stinking tavern! Yes: your uncle was a cheat, a liar, and a scoundrel! Too fine for work and ashamed of me because I was a lady's maid before he condescended to wed me for my savings."

"When did he die?" I could not resist asking.

"About ten years ago, and when he died I went through his papers which until then he had kept locked away in an old tin trunk. Only then did I discover that what he had told me of his boyhood was true: that he came of wealthy folk! That was when I began to make my plans. First I must re-marry so that my son and I should have a roof over our heads: my second husband was a man old enough to be my father but in his way he was good to us, and when he too died he left sufficient funds to enable Bernard and me to make our leisurely way back to England. We travelled across Europe: that was where we decided to reside permanently if our plans should come to fruition. Now, what was once only a remote possibility is an accomplished fact. For ten long years I have waited, but it was worth it. I have been patient, have I not?"

"But you could have written to Drawbridge Court!" I said. "There was no need for you to wed again just for the sake of security. My grandfather would have seen that neither you nor your son lacked for anything!"

"I could, but we should have been poor relations living on charity for the rest of our lives! No, my dear, my way is best for us. We have had to wait, but we shall get it all! I think we deserve it. All the rest of you have had your share of fine living. Your grandfather had nearly reached his three score years and ten when I helped him to depart this vale of tears!"

"You? You killed my darling Grandpapa?" My blood turned to ice.

"It was simplicity itself! I am a crack-shot, and I could hardly miss the drunken old fool with a shotgun at point-blank range!"

"My God!" I whispered. "Have you no pity? No remorse?"

"Those are luxuries which the rich and idle can afford. I too might cultivate those niceties when I am in the happy position to do so. The chimney-pot would have finished the business nicely if it had not been for that damned yapping cur of yours."

"But how did your son get into the house? Why was he not seen? I presume it was he who pushed it on to my aunt and me!"

"My son? Oh, no, it was I who contrived that! As you have remarked, I am agile; and the footprints which I was forced to leave behind were taken for those of a man, as I thought they would be. Who would suspect Mrs Ambrose?"

"You came to our house with murder in your heart!" I exclaimed. "You ate our bread and slept beneath our roof, and yet planned to kill us! You must be mad! You will never succeed in what you attempt!"

"So far all has gone well for us. We were prepared to leave your Uncle James until later, but as you had survived the accident with the chimney and the one in Rochester, I thought it would be best to turn our attentions elsewhere. There, my son was a great help! He knows a little of chemistry, so I left the matter in his hands. All I had to do was admit him to the house on the night before the explosion. He told me it was easy to create a gas which would explode when a flame was introduced into the chamber where it lay. Something about dripping water on to some element, carbide, I believe he said, would cause a low-lying gas to form: but as one walked amongst it carrying a lighted lamp or candle it would rise, meet the flame and, *voilà*!" The monster actually laughed!

"You fiend!" My blood, which had run so cold, now went coursing through my veins as fury took the place of fear. There was a red mist before my eyes as I sprang at her; to claw and scratch, and attempt to even bite! I could now understand murder; but this in my heart was of a different kind from that so carefully planned by this evil creature revelling in her wickedness. She had killed my loved ones, and now she was about to murder me! Well, my strength was puny when compared with that of these two devils; but even if they did bring me to my death, which it seemed was more than likely, I would mark her for the rest of her life before they did so! She would carry scars to her grave, I vowed!

"Let her be, Ma! There is no sense in harming her here. We might have to carry her back to the cliffs, and she looks to be a weighty piece!" Once more he hurled me to the floor and through my tousled hair I glared at the pair of them.

"I did not start it. She attacked me!" his mother protested.

"Where is that bag of hers? I can't see it! She did not drop it on the way here, did she?" Bernard demanded.

"I do not know! Stand up, you! Where is your reticule?"

But I remained where I was on the floor! Weighty piece, was I? They would find out just how weighty I was when they came to move me!

"It is not here! You had better go back and look for it."

"You should have seen her drop it! You were walking behind us," my cousin informed his mother angrily.

She prodded me with the toe of her boot.

"Where did you drop it, you bitch?" she shouted.

I did not know, but even if I did I would not tell them. The fury in my eyes must have matched the malice in hers for resolution, and she bent and dealt me a blow on the face with the back of her hand that sent my head backwards to meet the wall with a sickening thud. Indeed, I felt the vomit rise in my throat, but still I out-glared her.

"Never mind that. I shall soon find it," my cousin said, and I was left alone with his evil mother.

"As you are so happy to boast of your iniquity, perhaps you will tell me how you came to enter our employ?" I asked her.

"By pure chance, really. But if I had not come to Drawbridge Court as lady-companion, I should have done so in some other capacity. It was when I saw the advertisement in *The Times* that I knew it was the opportunity for which I had been waiting."

"So your references were forgeries!" I exclaimed.

"Oh, no, they were genuine enough, but they belonged to a woman other than myself. The careless creature was unfortunate enough to lose them and they found they way into my safe keeping," she mocked.

"But my aunt and I selected a Miss Johnson to fill the position. Even then you were only second best!" I could not resist adding.

The shot went home, and I had the satisfaction of seeing my tormentor flush angrily.

"Miss Johnson met with a slight accident: not so severe as those which your relatives have suffered, but sufficiently disabling to prevent her taking up her duties with you!"

"And so now you plan to ape the lady!" I scoffed. "A low-born serving wench will attempt to pass herself off for gentry!"

"You forget that I have already done so for over a year! As a lady's maid I was well acquainted with what is expected of the so-called upper classes: and my worthless but fastidious husband was always swift to deride any slight mistake which I once made. No, I think I shall pass very well! Anyway, a wealthy woman is allowed to behave eccentrically if she chooses: a fat enough purse will excuse any social gaffe!"

Once more it was raining, and the light inside the building in which I was a prisoner had become dim. I did not know whether this was caused by the massed black clouds overhead, or the fact that darkness was beginning to fall. The conversation that had just taken place seemed to have lulled my gaoler into a sense of security: she was not so alert as she had been, and was standing with hands in greatcoat pockets contemplating the toe of her riding boot. Now was my chance to make a dash for freedom: if I moved quickly enough I might reach the doorway before she could stop me! Even if she did, at the moment we were one against one, although she was far stronger than I; but if I hesitated her son would return and my opportunity would be gone. I tensed the muscles in my legs ready to sprint across the chamber, but even as I did so I knew I was too late. There was the sound of someone forcing his way through the hedge as we had done, and in the doorway appeared the man who, whether he was or not, I called Luker! I was not really surprised to see him: although no mention had been made of him I was already convinced that he in some way had aided them in their villainy, then,

"I found this fellow nosing about in the meadow!" Bernard was behind Luker, pistol in hand, and he thrust the man forward so that he must stagger to regain his balance. "He said he was taking a walk, but I think there might be more reason than that for him being where I found him!"

"Who is he?" my odious aunt asked. "His face is familiar, but I cannot put a name to it!"

Mercifully, I had the sense to keep my tongue between my teeth. If these evil creatures did not know whom it was they had caught, he could not be a party to their wickedness.

"He says he is a tourist on holiday, but I do not like the looks of him!"

All this time Luker had stood mumchance: I tried to catch his eye, but resolutely he looked in any direction but mine.

"You have done well to find him, whoever he is. Did you discover the bag?"

"No. We shall have to look for that as we go. It is time we went, anyway. The tide will be in soon, but we want some of the rocks to still be exposed to make sure: if they are all covered by the sea it could be a chancy business. Our friend here will have to join the tragic party."

"One who attempted a rescue in vain? Yes: I like the sound of that. It is neat!"

Horrified, I stared from one to the other.

"You cannot do that!" I whispered. "Not to a completely innocent stranger! I can understand the way your crazed minds work so far as I am concerned, but this man has done you no harm!"

"He could though, could he not, if he were allowed to go free? Come, on your feet! It is time we went," was the callous reply.

Defiantly, I sat and stared up at them. What would happen if I refused to move? There could be nothing worse than death, and that was a certainty if I obliged them by walking to my doom. Bernard wished for the foul deed to be done whilst some of the rocks were still exposed: if I could delay them until the tide had covered these same rocks, would Luker and I gain a little time? It was obvious that my aunt and cousin wanted our bodies to be dashed upon the rocks at the foot of the cliffs and then when the tide receded, to be carried out to sea. If the sea was already covering the rocks when Luker and I were thrown from the cliff-tops it was not certain that we should be killed. Although it was unlikely that we might swim to safety or be spied by a fishing-boat, it was possible! I folded my arms and determinedly, I continued to sit!

"Up, damn you!" A vicious kick which landed on my thigh brought tears to my eyes, but still I would not move; though my resolve soon weakened as his mother said:

"Stand aside. I will shift her!" and did so by the simple expedient of grasping a handful of my hair and jerking it upwards. If I had remained where I was my hair would have been torn out by the roots; so I was brutally bought to my feet and thrust out into the steadily falling rain.

The short journey thence-forward was of a nightmare quality: delay was still uppermost in my mind, and every pace that I took had to be forced from me by a kick or a buffet. It wanted only a small amount of this treatment to make me wonder whether the punishment I was receiving was worth the very slight chance that in some way we might yet be saved. The muscles in my legs ached intolerably: I was soon suffering from the pain of the savage blows which were continuously compelling me forward, ever forward! I was in the charge of my infamous aunt, whilst my cousin kept Luker covered by the pistol.

Closer and closer came the place from where we would be launched into eternity. There were no seagulls to be heard now: only the boom of the surging tide far, far below. The wind had increased to gale force, and I wondered half-heartedly how far I should get if I tried to run for my life. Would Bernard shoot me down? He might hesitate to do so, for a bullet wound would not easily be explained in the corpse of somebody presumed to have fallen over a cliff!

Once more I was too late. With fingers like steel my aunt took my arm to force me to the cliff edge. Oh, how I fought her! I dug my heels into the ground upon which we were struggling, but my feet could find no purchase in the slippery mud. Like an animal I clawed and kicked! Civilized behaviour had no place here upon the cliff, this was a fight for survival; all of my basic instincts rebelling against the fate which soon must be mine if I was conquered. She was more powerfully built than I, and although from somewhere I found a strength to resist her which amazed me, slowly she began to overpower me. Like primitive creatures we were locked in mortal combat: to the victor went life and liberty, but to the vanquished, death!

Then from somewhere, above the crash of the waves and the howl of the gale, came the crack of a pistol shot! Poor Luker I thought, but I was mistaken! My Aunt Helen, as startled as I, momentarily released her hold upon me and glanced around in the direction from where the shot was fired. Dreading to look yet knowing I must, I too peered through the falling rain to see what had happened: and what I saw instead of sickening me as I had feared, sent a flood of relief and thankfulness coursing through my entire being. Help was at hand, and we were saved!

The horseman who approached was riding at such a pace that it put himself and his mount in grave danger; nay, there was not one horseman, there were two!

"Quick, Ma, run for it!"

Gallant as ever, my cousin left his mother to make what speed she could as he turned inland, and fled in the direction of the ruined building and his waiting horses. The foremost rider came straight on to Luker and me, but the other turned aside to frustrate the attempted escape of Bernard and my loathsome aunt. Like a sheep-dog rounding up his flock he brought them back in our direction, and I turned my attention from them to the foremost horseman, who was by now dismounting. It was Perry! My darling had come in time to snatch me from the jaws of death, but now stood in dire peril himself!

"Be careful! He has a pistol!" I shrieked, but my warning was unnecessary. It was very evident that my cousin had a pistol and would have no compunction in using it: in fact I fleetingly wondered why he had not done so already.

"Fear not, my love, so has Mr Rumbold!" This must be the other rescuer, and by now he had the flagitious pair standing near the cliff edge a little way from where stood Luker, Perry and I.

"Cast down your weapon!" Mr Rumbold shouted to my cousin, and as one in a dream I recognized Mr Rumbold as the gentleman in brown; the man whom I had noticed so often in the streets of Broadstairs!

"Never! Come any closer and I will fire!"

"No, don't, he will kill you!" I screeched as Mr Rumbold disregarded the threat and spurred his horse towards the cornered miscreants. They stood at bay: their full attention upon the man who was about to ride them down, and in dreadful fascination I watched as seemingly involuntarily they took first one pace backwards and then another until no more than a distance of two feet separated them from the very brink of the cliff. They could go no further, and now Bernard must surrender his pistol, himself and his mother to justice!

I breathed a sigh of relief as I saw him throw down his weapon, but my sigh changed to a scream of pure horror as I watched the ground upon which they had made their last stand crumble beneath their feet! One moment they were there, and the next they were gone; with only their cries of terror to ring and echo in my ears long after they had disappeared from sight. This last ghastly shock robbed me of the little strength I had left, and I fell to my knees in the trampled mud and buried my face in my hands. For a brief moment I attempted to erase from my mind the howling gale and the lashing rain: the unspeakable afternoon which I had survived: the macabre revelations which had been made to me, and the bone weariness of my aching and bruised body. My teeth began to chatter and my limbs to shake, and try as I would I could control neither, until two strong arms enfolded me and held me close.

"There, there, my love! It is all over. You are safe, my little queen, my precious one. There now, just rest awhile. No, do not attempt to rise for a moment or two. Stay here in my arms for as long as you wish!"

Gradually the tremors left my body and I peeped over my beloved's shoulder to see Luker and Mr Rumbold standing at a safe distance from the edge of the cliff, gazing seawards.

"I am all right now," I whispered, and then I realized that the two of us were kneeling in the mud and that it was almost dark: the gale was blowing harder than ever and the rain was still descending in torrents to soak us to the skin; whilst the waves far below boomed menacingly against the cliff face.

"Are you sure, my darling? We shall stay here until you are recovered somewhat from your ordeal."

"No, let us depart from this dreadful place," I said. "Please, Perry, take me away from here!"

He called the two men and it was arranged that they should take the horses which were with us and go to fetch the other two poor beasts which were still tethered at the back of the ruin which had served as my prison for the afternoon. Even if we had not needed them as mounts, we could not have left the helpless animals to die from starvation and lack of water. Perry and I walked ahead whilst this errand was despatched, but when our party had a mount for each person I found I was still too afflicted by shock and injury to even consider riding.

"I shall carry you to safety on my saddle-bow," my darling said as he mounted. "Just as the knights did in days of yore. Mr Rumbold, pray assist Miss Kimberley to take her place in front of me."

And so I nestled against his heart with his arm firm

about me as we made our careful way back to Broadstairs, but before we reached Pierremont Avenue I recovered myself sufficiently to say:

"Aunt Sylvia must never know the truth of what transpired this afternoon!"

"Well, my love, I cannot tell her for I do not know what it is," Perry replied fondly.

"Let us say there has been an accident, and that Mrs Ambrose and a gentleman who tried to save her have fallen over the cliffs. I am too weary to elaborate further, but that is the best explanation of which I can think at the moment. Tomorrow I shall tell you all that has passed this terrible day, but now, my darling, all I feel capable of doing is falling asleep!"

TEN

It was after noon when I awoke next day. For a brief moment I wondered why every bone in my body ached, and why I felt so dreadfully tired: then remembrance of the events of the day before came flooding back to me, and though my tender flesh rebelled I struggled into a sitting position and rang my bell. Aunt Sylvia, Bertha and Carlin were with me almost immediately: Aunt Sylvia to straighten my bedcovers and plump my pillows: Bertha to depart for my tea-tray; and Carlin to greet me vociferously and refuse to still his barking until he was lifted up beside me on to my bed.

"Oh, my dear child, how are you feeling? When he brought you home Peregrine assured me that you had suffered no more than cuts and bruises, and he suggested that you would not welcome it if I sent for the doctor to attend you."

"He was quite right," I replied. "I am very stiff and sore, but my injuries are trivial when compared to the fate of Mrs Ambrose and that of the young man who was with us. Did Perry tell you what happened?"

"Yes, so far as he was able. Of course, as he was not with you when the accident occurred all he knew was what you had told him: and you were in such a parlous state that he refrained from questioning you too closely. Can you bear to speak of what befell, or would you rather wait until you feel stronger?"

"I will tell you now," I answered. "It is only right that you should know what happened, straightaway.

The path was very slippery and when the rain started to fall once more, Mrs Ambrose and I decided to shelter for a while. The walk had been more tiring than either of us had expected and we were glad to rest; but when the rain showed no sign of abating we elected to continue on our way to Ramsgate. There was a young man whom we met as we resumed our journey, and he very gallantly helped us over the more difficult places to be traversed. Then we came to a section of the path which was very near to the cliff edge: it was narrow, so we had to proceed in single file. Mrs Ambrose went first, then the stranger, and I brought up the rear. The chalky ground crumbled beneath Mrs Ambrose's feet! As you know she was a heavily built woman, and I think that if the young man had not been brave enough to attempt to save her, he might have saved himself! I believe he caught hold of her as she fell, but the weight of her carried them both to their doom!"

"What a ghastly thing to happen!" Aunt Sylvia whispered. "Oh, the poor, dear lady, to lose her life in such a terrible way! I shall miss her dreadfully! She was the soul of kindness: ever amiable, ever helpful, and such good company! How we shall contrive without her I am sure I do not know!"

"Nor I," I replied gravely.

"But, my love, how came you by your injuries?" my aunt enquired, and I had to think quickly.

"To be quite truthful, I do not know with any degree of certainty," I hedged. "From the moment when they fell, things became a trifle blurred. I must have fallen myself! I may have tried to reach them in the vain hope that I could do something to aid them: I have no clear recollection of what befell after then; but Perry told me that when he found me I was lying a-swoon in the pouring rain, only inches from the brink of the cliff!"

Aunt Sylvia shuddered.

"Oh, Autumn, let us give thanks that you were saved!" she said. "I should have gone out of my mind with grief if you too had been taken from me! What harm have we done, that we must be dogged by such ill fortune? Will we ever know happy times again, I wonder?"

I took her hand and held it tightly.

"Yes," I replied, gently. "I think that although the sorrow which we bear will never free us completely from its grasp, we shall suffer no more heartache for a very long time to come!"

* * *

That Perry was to dine with us that evening was sufficient incentive for me to insist that I leave my bed, despite Aunt Sylvia's protests: and I assert that no young woman could have a sweeter aunt than mine, for directly the meal was over she complained of a headache, and nothing would serve but that she seek the seclusion of her chamber.

"I am so sorry, my dears, but I am afraid that I simply must leave you to entertain each other! Pray forgive me, but my headaches descend upon me without the slightest warning, and then there is nothing I can do but lie in a darkened room until they go away!"

Her voice was faint and the look of martyrdom on her face was most convincing; but I was quick enough to see her lips twitch and her eyes sparkle with glee at her own subtlety as she left the drawing-room. What a sly-boots she was; and oh, how I loved her!

As a flower turns to the sun so I turned to Perry, and without conscious volition we were in each other's arms. He held me close against his heart, then gently led me towards the glowing fire: there to seat me in a great armchair and ply me with cushions.

"Thank you, my darling," I said. "But if there were not so many cushions in this chair with me, and if we sit close together, there will be room for the two of us!"

And so with his arm around me and my head upon his shoulder, I sat and gazed dreamily into the fire.

"My love, loath as I am to spoil this wonderful moment, I fear I must do it. Tomorrow there will be questions to be answered and explanations to be made, and until you tell me what transpired yesterday afternoon I am afraid I can do neither. Luker has told me what he knows, but he cannot say what took place before he was taken to that ruin where those creatures were holding you prisoner."

"So it was Luker! I was certain that I had seen him in Broadstairs, but had almost convinced myself that I was mistaken. Who is he? And who is Mr Rumbold, the gentleman in brown? One or the other of them seemed to follow us wherever we went! They made me most uneasy: I was so sure they were planning devilry of some sort! No, that is not true: I was not sure, and that made me more uneasy than ever!"

Perry laughed aloud, then said:

"What a clumsy pair they must be! Or am I misjudging them? I warned them that you were a most astute young lady, but they assured me that you would not be aware of their presence. Oh, my darling, they are in my employ! I hired them to keep watch on your movements, and to protect you from harm! Even before you mentioned your fears to me I had become suspicious of the number of seeming accidents which were occurring at Drawbridge Court, and to its occupants. Rumbold and Luker are a pair of private detectives: Rumbold is an ex-policeman, and Luker is his assistant!"

"So that is how he came to be on the cliff-tops yesterday!" I exclaimed. "But that does not explain your presence there, nor that of Mr Rumbold! I did not expect to see you until today!"

"I hoped to surprise you by arriving a day early," Perry answered. "I did not break my journey, but travelled straight through from Derbyshire. Then I sent my valet and luggage on to the hotel and I lost no time in coming here, only to be told that you and Mrs Ambrose had gone out walking and that your aunt was taking a rest. Bitterly disappointed, I then went to my hotel to find Rumbold waiting to report to me: he knows my valet, and by chance he had seen him arriving at the hotel with my luggage and he guessed that I would not be far behind. Rumbold assured me that all was well with you: he and Luker had followed you and Mrs Ambrose to the west cliffs, and when you proceeded to set out in the direction of Ramsgate they had decided that Luker should follow and Rumbold should remain behind."

"Then you did not know I was in danger!" I said. "No, of course not! How could you?"

"Not at that time. I could not contain my impatience to see you, so I sent Rumbold to hire a horse for me so that I might ride to Ramsgate and meet you as you entered the town: there to give you tea, and escort you back to Broadstairs. Rumbold chose to bear me company, but when we reached Ramsgate and there was no sign of you, we began to grow uneasy. Rain had started to fall and we waited and waited, and still you did not appear: then I knew beyond any shadow of doubt that something was amiss! What endangered you I did not know: I only knew that I must ride along the cliff path if I was to save you! Never before have I believed in premonitions, but now I do: some force which there was no denying drove me and my beast forward, and Rumbold faithfully followed. The rest you know!"

"Ah, yes, I do! I shall always remember that moment when I saw you appear through the driving rain, but now I will tell you my tale, and you will be able to see how it all came about."

Carefully I chose my words and tried to keep my voice free from emotion; but when I related how Mrs Ambrose had gloried in her wickedness, and how she had laughed when she had told me how simple it had been to send my beloved grandsire and uncle to their deaths, my self-restraint left me and I wept. With Perry's arms tight about me I sobbed out the rest of my story, and when I had finished, for a short while he was silent. His face was grim when next he spoke.

"My God, I know that wickedness exists in the world, but never did I think it could come so close to the one whom I love above all others! You have lived with evil personified for over a year! At any time you might have been slain! My blood runs cold at the thought of it!"

"I have survived, but I have lost my dear ones," I whispered. "You see why Aunt Sylvia must never be told the truth of what happened? She is getting over the worst of her grief for Uncle James and Grandpapa, but I think the shock of knowing that the woman of whom she thinks so highly is responsible for their deaths, would kill her! Somehow we must contrive to keep the dreadful facts from her, though how we shall do it I do not know!"

"Rumbold will be able to assist us in that direction I am certain," Perry assured me. "He has a little influence, even though he has retired from the police force. Between us we will get this ghastly business sorted out and kept quiet, and then I will spend the rest of my life in helping you to forget the unhappiness which you have suffered."

"Oh, my love, what should I do without you?" I murmured.

"That you shall never know, for from this day forward you will never be free of me. We shall be married at once! Nay, do not attempt to protest! In three weeks' time we shall be wed, here in Broadstairs. I will not have another easy moment until I know you are my wife: to love and honour, to cherish and protect. For all of my life I have loved you: I have loved you as a little maid, I have loved you as a schoolroom miss; and now that the beautiful bud of youth has opened into the glorious flower of womanhood, I worship the very ground you walk upon! Oh, my darling, my heart's desire; I beseech you, do not make me wait any longer for the right to proclaim to the world that you are mine!"

Our lips met and I was lost: once more I was a prisoner, but this time it was in the embrace of my beloved, and to endure such captivity for the rest of my life was my dearest wish.